THE
LONG RIDE
H◆ME

SUSAN R. LAWRENCE

journeyforth®

Greenville, South Carolina

Library of Congress Cataloging-in Publication Data
Names: Lawrence, Susan, 1950- author. | Hutcheon, Nathan, illustrator.
Title: The long ride home / Susan R. Lawrence ; Illustrations by Nathan
    Hutcheon.
Description: Greenville, South Carolina : JourneyForth, [2017] |
    Summary: Hoping to find a family, Bert Davidson, accompanied by his
    younger sister
Emma, boards an orphan train for Iowa in 1929 and learns some eternal
truths as he attends a one-room school and works on a farm.
Identifiers: LCCN 2017025719 (print) | LCCN 2017037392 (ebook) |
    ISBN 9781628564464 (ebook) | ISBN 9781628564457 (perfect bound
    pbk. : alk. paper)
Subjects: | CYAC: Orphans—Fiction. | Orphan trains—Fiction. | Adoption
    Fiction. | Farm life—Iowa—Fiction. | Christian life—Fiction. | Iowa—
    History—20th century—Fiction.
Classification: LCC PZ7.1.L389 (ebook) | LCC PZ7.1.L389 Lo 2017
    (print) | DDC [Fic]—dc23
LC record available at https://lccn.loc.gov/2017025719

All Scripture is quoted from the King James Version.

Illustrations and design by Nathan Hutcheon
Page layout by Michael Boone

© 2017 BJU Press
Greenville, South Carolina 29609-5046
JourneyForth Books is a division of BJU Press.

ISBN 978-1-62856-445-7
eISBN 978-1-62856-446-4

15   14   13   12   11   10   9   8   7   6   5   4   3   2   1

CONTENTS

CHAPTER 1

New York City, 1929

I felt the train before I saw it. The wooden floor of the depot trembled. The whistle sounded twice, a long, mournful sound. Then the whole building shook as the train rumbled into view.

My little sister, Emma, slid closer to me on the bench and clutched my hand. I couldn't let her know I was terrified too. I lowered my head and whispered, "You'll be okay. I'll take care of you."

Mr. Carter, the social worker from the Children's Aid Society who would accompany us to Oak Hill, stood and clapped his hands sharply. The row of twelve children, including Emma and me, fastened our eyes on him. "We will be boarding the train in a few minutes. I want you to stay with your partner and follow me." His hawk-like eyes lit on a few of the older boys. "No shenanigans." Then he glared at me. "Bert Davidson, don't forget your bag."

I reached under the bench for the sack that held a new blue shirt, a change of underwear, and a clean pair of socks. Mr. Carter gave them to me yesterday when he told me that Emma and I, along with ten other children, would ride the train west from New York City. We would travel to new lives in a place I'd never heard of before, Iowa. There, if our luck held out, we would meet a family who would take us in. We would no longer be orphans. I clutched the bag to my chest as we lined up single file behind Mr. Carter.

I checked to make sure Emma had her bag. She'd told me all about the dress tucked inside it. She said it was yellow with some kind of flowers all over. Probably the first new dress she'd ever had. Emma would look real pretty in it. Maybe as pretty as Mama.

Emma didn't remember Mama, but I did. She wore her dark hair all swept up on top of her head, and she always smelled like roses. But after she got sick, her face grew pale and her hair spread out around her on the pillow. Then, if I bent to kiss her cheek, she smelled like medicine.

The line of children stopped, and I bumped into Ruth who stood in front of me. She turned with a cross look on her face, but when she saw Emma she just said, "Watch where you're going."

"Sorry," I mumbled. The line moved again, out the door and across the wooden platform. Up close the train looked huge. Papa always called the trains *iron horses*. I didn't even like horses. Once I reached out to pet a horse hitched to a peddler's cart, and the animal bit me.

Mr. Carter stepped up and handed the uniformed man some papers. After a brief conversation with him, Mr. Carter moved in and beckoned the children to follow. As we walked up the stairs, the train conductor touched each head and counted aloud.

We walked through several cars where other passengers sat until Mr. Carter stopped in a doorway and turned to face us. "This is our car. You will sit with your partner.

Your bags go under your seat. If both partners want to sit by the window, you will take turns. There is a bathroom in the rear of the car. After the train is moving, you may get up and use it. But when you are not using the restroom, I expect you to stay seated. There will be no horseplay."

His piercing gaze demanded a response, and without exception all of us nodded. "Yes, Mr. Carter," we chorused.

Emma tugged on my hand. "Bert, let's sit here. Let's sit here." She bounced across the seat to the window and pressed her nose to the glass.

I stuffed our bags under the seat and stared out the window. For as far as I could see, there were only buildings—tall ones and short ones, new, shiny ones, and old, shabby ones.

This was the only city I'd ever known. I'd been born here, and after Mama died and Pa disappeared, I'd roamed its streets searching for jobs where I could make a few pennies to buy food for Emma and me. When the Children's Aid workers arrived at the door and took us to the orphanage, most of what I felt was relief. Emma wouldn't have to cry again because she was hungry.

The train shuddered, then with a series of noisy clicks, it inched forward. Faster and faster and faster. It seemed to be singing a song. *Leaving New York City. Leaving New York City.*

I leaned past Emma and watched as the buildings flew past. At first I recognized a few of them and then all was strange and new. Tall apartment buildings with clotheslines strung across the back porches waved their clean laundry. Factories spewed smoke that clouded the window Emma stared out of. Where the tracks intersected a road, cars lined up, motors chugging as they waited for the train to pass. Emma always waved at them, and sometimes a driver's hand would thrust out the window, waving in return.

When lunchtime came, Mr. Carter handed each of us a sandwich wrapped in waxed paper, a small bottle of milk, and an apple.

"Don't spill your milk, Emma," I cautioned.

"I won't." Emma turned to the window again, and milk sloshed out onto her dress. "Oops. Sorry." Her blue eyes filled with tears.

I sighed. No napkins. I pulled out the handkerchief Miss Carmichael had handed me before we left the Children's Aid Society this morning. I blotted up the spill as best I could, then took the bottle from her and wedged it between my legs next to my bottle. "All cleaned up. Now just tell me when you need a drink, and I'll hold it for you."

"Thanks, Bert." Tears gone, she smiled up at me. The smile that nearly always made me give in to whatever she wanted. Little sisters could be pests, but all we had was each other, and I was going to take care of her no matter what.

After we ate, Emma had to use the restroom. I walked to the rear of the car with her and stood outside the little room until she came back out. We peered through the connector into the next car. It was a dining car where, if you had money, you could sit at a table and order any food you wanted.

A waiter in white clothes carrying a tray of dirty dishes made a shooing motion at us and shouted through the passageway. "You children go back into your car. You don't belong in here."

We hurried back to our seat. Within a few minutes, Emma's head began nodding and then slid toward my shoulder. Watching her sleep made me yawn, but I didn't want to miss any part of this trip. So I forced my eyes to stay open.

Outside the window the rows of towering apartments were gone. Long stretches of trees and fields sometimes gave way to city streets lined with houses. I wondered what the houses looked like and if each one had a family inside.

When I had to use the restroom, I leaned Emma over and laid her head on the arm rest. She didn't even wake up. Mr. Carter's nose was buried in a newspaper, but he looked up as I passed. "Going to use the bathroom?"

I nodded. "Yes, sir." But Mr. Carter had already turned back to the paper. I wished I had something to read, maybe a comic strip like I'd found once in the trash can or the storybook Mama had read me about Robin Hood and his merry men.

I passed the two rows of older boys. Frank Pearson sneered up at me. "Still nursemaiding yer little sister, Bert?"

I hurried past like I didn't hear. After I used the restroom, I closed the door and started back up the aisle, looking to see if Emma was awake. Suddenly my body sprawled the length of three seats, and my chin scraped the floor. Heads swiveled to stare at me, and some of the kids laughed. Frank pulled his foot, the one I'd tripped over, back in front of him.

Mr. Carter rose to his feet. "What's going on back there?"

I glanced at Frank's smirking face. Then I stood up and brushed off my pants. "I just stumbled."

Frank whispered, "Get up there in the front and take care of your baby, Sissy Boy."

My hands fisted at my side, but I took a deep breath and walked back to my seat. I'd get back at him later.

CHAPTER 2

By afternoon, the houses became fewer and farther between. We traveled through a forest with tall pine trees crowding the train on either side. And we passed fields with more grass than I'd ever seen in one place. Once Emma nudged me and pointed. Several large black and white animals stared at the train from behind a fence.

"Those are cows, Emma." I told her, hoping I was right. The only cows I'd seen before were pictures in a book. I pressed against her shoulder, watching until the animals disappeared from sight.

Supper was a repeat of lunch. And shortly after, Mr. Carter handed out thin, scratchy blankets to all the children.

Emma pulled me down to whisper. "Should I say my prayers now?"

"Sure." I listened as she recited the prayer I'd taught her, the prayer I used to say.

"Now I lay me down to sleep. I pray the Lord my soul to keep. If I should die before I wake, I pray the Lord my soul to take. God bless Bert. God bless Miss Carmichael. And help us find a new family."

Then Emma pulled her blanket to her chin, snuggled against my arm, and promptly fell asleep.

I stayed awake for a long time, listening to the steady click of the wheels and the soft snores of the children around me. Maybe I should pray too. When I was Emma's age, Mama sat on the edge of my bed and listened to me pray. Did God hear us so far from New York? Would He really help us find a family?

I didn't remember falling asleep, but, after what seemed like only a few minutes, my eyes opened. The windows were bright squares in the dim light of the train car. When I stretched around my sleeping sister to stare out our window, I could see the bright ball of the sun creeping up over the fields. I drew in my breath and let it out slowly. I'd never seen anything so pretty. In New York we didn't see the sun until midmorning when it finally rose above the towering buildings around us. Should I wake Emma so she could see it too? Then her eyelids blinked open. One hand poked out from under the blanket, and she rubbed her eyes. I pointed out the window without speaking.

She sat up and turned to gaze out. "Oh, Bert, I've never seen the sun turn on. Look. My favorite color."

And she was right. The rising sun tinted the feathery clouds the same shade of pink as cotton candy. We both watched as the color faded and the world brightened.

"I need to use the restroom." Emma wiggled out of her blanket and stood up.

"I'll take you." I didn't want to walk past the older boys, Frank in particular, but I sure didn't want my little sister to face them alone. The boys were still sleeping, so we both used the restroom, then returned to our seats.

The changing scenery out the window still fascinated me, but Emma wanted to talk.

"We get to Iowa tomorrow, don't we?"

"That's what Mr. Carter said."

"What will it be like? Will it look like this?" She pointed her finger in the direction of the window, where fields stretched in every direction.

"Probably."

"Will we meet our new family tomorrow, Bert? Will they be nice?"

I sighed and shrugged. "Enough questions. I haven't ever been to Iowa. I don't know what it's like, except there's lots of farms. That's why all those older boys are on this train. They're hoping to get jobs. And we don't know if we'll get a new family. Mr. Carter may just have to haul us back to New York." Part of me secretly hoped that would happen. I knew life in New York. Everything in Iowa was foreign.

The morning flew by as fast as the fields outside the train window. Sometimes we stopped in a small town. While we watched out the window, passengers stepped from the train. Often there were people on the platform who greeted them, hugging and kissing. Those were families, I guessed. I imagined myself grown, coming home on a train, and a mom and dad meeting me. But as hard as I tried, I couldn't picture their faces.

When the train whistle blew and the wheels began their clickety-clack once more, I studied the farms. White houses with broad porches looked small beside big red barns. Fences stretched on in all directions like huge playpens for the animals. Cows and horses, pigs and chickens scattered when the train rumbled past.

By afternoon everyone was tired of sitting, tired of watching fields out the window, and tired of wondering about Iowa. Arguments broke out among the children. Mr. Carter stood up, barked crossly, and threatened to make us go without supper. When darkness arrived, everyone seemed grateful to pull blankets up and sleep.

When I woke the next morning, my first thought was *this is the day. This is the day we'll get to Iowa.* Emma squirmed in her seat and opened her eyes. "Are we in Iowa?"

"No, but we will be today."

We watched the sunrise and more fields and farms and cows. The closer we got to Iowa, the more my stomach hurt. What if no one wanted me? What if no one wanted Emma?

She slumped against the window, her eyes closed. I didn't know if she was sleeping or bored.

When Mr. Carter handed out sandwiches and milk at lunchtime, I nudged her awake. Her blue eyes opened wide, and she sat up. "Are we in Iowa yet?"

"I don't think so, but I can't tell." I handed her a sandwich. I took a huge bite of my peanut butter and bread and washed it down with a swig from my bottle of milk.

Emma unwrapped her sandwich, but didn't eat. Maybe she was nervous too.

"Eat your lunch, Emma. It's good food that Shirley packed." Shirley, the cook at the Children's Aid Society, always had an extra cookie for my tray or a kind word and a smile. Emma nibbled at the edge of her crust.

I thought about not seeing Shirley again or Miss Carmichael, who took care of the girls, or even Pa. He'd run out on us, and I hadn't expected to see him in New York, but I knew I'd never see him in Iowa.

Mr. Carter came down the aisle with a sack, collecting the papers from the sandwiches and the empty milk bottles. When he reached the front of the car, he clapped his hands. "We should be arriving at Oak Hill in the next few hours. We'll be met by the committee who has made arrangements for us. The Mason Hotel is providing dinner and a place to clean up, and then we will meet prospective families at the opera house. I don't think I need to remind you how important it is for you to be on your best behavior." He glared at us for a minute before picking up the sack and moving back to his seat.

"What's *spective families*?" Emma asked.

"The families that want an orphan." I leaned back and closed my eyes. I didn't want to think about it, and I didn't want to answer any more of my sister's questions.

CHAPTER 3

The engine hissed, and the train slowed. We passed white houses with wide porches, large back yards, and trees not yet leafed out. As we slid to a stop, buildings appeared. Not the towering skyscrapers of New York, but sturdy two-story brick structures that sat like upended boxes along the street.

A crowd of people stood on the platform, their eyes on the train. A sign on the end of the small depot declared this was Oak Hill. I nudged Emma with my elbow. "We're in Iowa now."

We must have crossed the state line a few hours before, but this was the place in Iowa that mattered. The town where someone would decide whether Emma and I would stay orphans or not.

Mr. Carter marched down to the front of the car. He didn't even have to clap his hands for our attention. All eyes fastened on him, and no one dared whisper. "We will be the last car to exit. Don't forget your bags. We will meet the committee from Oak Hill, and they will escort us to the hotel."

Through the window, I could see people stepping off the train. A few hurried away, but many joined the waiting crowd. My whole body tensed, like the times in New York when I'd searched through garbage cans for scraps of food. I'd watched the back doors of the restaurants for someone to come out and holler at me or even call the police.

Mr. Carter picked up his bags. "Follow me." Without looking behind him, he exited the car. Children popped up from their seats like puppets and joined the line.

Emma held her bag close to her and grabbed my arm with her other hand. "Don't let me go."

For a minute I thought she meant she didn't want to leave the train and then I understood. I took her hand. "I'll hold on real tight. We won't let anyone separate us."

On the platform the crowd of people stirred and murmured. Someone shouted, "Here they come."

"Look at the little girl. Isn't she sweet?" I wanted to stare at the person who spoke, but I kept my eyes on Mr. Carter. Without looking I knew Emma's eyes were glued on me. Mr. Carter paused, and the children behind him bumped to a stop.

When a group of two men and two women stepped forward, Mr. Carter talked with them, sometimes gesturing back at us. Then the five adults stepped down from the platform, and we children trailed after.

We'd only walked about half a block when the adults stopped in front of the largest brick building on the street. Over the door was a sign that said Mason Hotel.

Inside I stared upward at the huge chandelier with sparkling glass and real electric lights. I wished it was dark so I could see the lights come on. I finally pulled my gaze from the chandelier and looked around the room. Plush chairs were grouped in front of a fireplace. A wide staircase led to a second story. Upstairs a row of closed doors looked over a balcony.

A boy about my age leaned over the railing and pointed at us. "Look, Ma, there they are. The orphans are here." I wished I could hide behind someone like Emma seemed to be trying to do. I pulled her up beside me.

"Don't be a fraidy cat. Stand up here."

Emma took one step forward, but her eyes were large and filled with fear. After the adults talked for what seemed like a very long time, the man behind the desk handed Mr. Carter a key. We followed Mr. Carter up the wide stairs. One of the women from the platform trailed behind the line of children.

Thankfully, there was no sign of the boy. He must have disappeared behind one of the doors. Mr. Carter used his key to unlock the door marked 201. Inside were a bed, a chair, a washstand, and a door that must have led to another room.

"We'll change clothes here and tidy up. We don't have time for everyone to have a bath, but you can wash your hands and faces. Mrs. Johnson will take the girls in that room." Mr. Carter pointed to the door of the adjoining room.

Ruth, Ann Marie, and another smaller girl followed the committee woman. I pried Emma's fingers off my hand. "You have to go now. Follow the girls. I'll be right here. Put on your pretty dress."

Watching me over her shoulder, she trudged after the other girls, the sack containing her dress dragging on the floor.

After the door closed between the two rooms, Mr. Carter lined the boys up. "Wash up first, then put on your clean shirts. I have a couple combs for your hair."

Fred, who stood ahead of me in the line, whispered, "Don't know why we older boys have to clean up. We're just trying to get a job on a farm."

I nodded agreement. "This shirt's just fine." But I moved to the stand and used one of the washcloths to scrub at my face, remembering how Mama always said, "Wash behind your ears."

After everyone had cleaned up and Mr. Carter had checked our hands and necks and hair, we filed back down the stairs and into the dining room. Spotless white tablecloths covered the tables set with white plates and shiny silverware. Even though I'd washed up, I wiped my hands on my pants. I wished I were back in New York, getting ready to eat some of Shirley's food.

Mr. Carter indicated which tables were ours, and I took the empty chair next to Fred.

In a few minutes the girls fluttered in. Emma spotted me and skipped over. She whirled around, her skirt spreading out around her like one of the morning glories that climbed the fence in the empty lot.

"My dress, Bert. See my new dress?" Her face showed no trace of her previous fear.

"Emma, dear, come and sit down in your chair." The tall slender woman Mr. Carter had called Mrs. Johnson stood behind an empty chair, and Emma pranced over. Someone had brushed her hair and tied two yellow ribbons on the sides.

Across the table Frank and Jim were quiet, without their usual elbow jabs and snide comments. A door swished open and several white shirted men entered the dining room with huge round trays on their shoulders. They set the trays on stands and then began unloading plates and bowls of food. One plate was piled high with golden-brown, crispy chicken.

Fred whispered, "Think it's as good as Shirley's?"

I shook my head, but my mouth watered just a little. I couldn't wait to find out.

The bowls held mounds of fluffy mashed potatoes with butter running like lava down the sides, and applesauce that looked cool and smooth. Baskets lined with more white cloths held biscuits with golden tops and bottoms and middles white as the clouds in the Iowa sky. I reached for a biscuit just as Mrs. Johnson stood and cleared her throat.

"On behalf of the Oak Grove Orphan Committee, I would like to welcome all of you. Of course, we're especially glad to see you children." She paused and gazed around at all of us, beaming. "The Mason Hotel has provided this meal for all free of charge. Before we eat, I'd like to offer grace."

I bowed my head and closed my eyes. But Mrs. Johnson's words were like the drone of the traffic on the New York streets, and I didn't really hear a word until the *Amen.*

Then I snatched a biscuit out of the basket before passing it to Fred. The platter of chicken had been placed between Frank and Jim, so when it got to me, there were no more drumsticks. I pulled a crispy, golden thigh out and put it on my plate, and, because no adults were watching, I took a second piece, a wing.

I'd just bitten into that juicy thigh when Frank leaned across the table. "So, Sissy Boy, you think anyone's going to pick you?"

The thigh thumped back onto my plate. "Well, yeah. I hope so. I mean, Emma and I, we'd be good kids." Sounded kinda silly even to me. I knew Frank wouldn't just sit back and let me be.

Frank's face screwed up like he'd sucked a lemon. "Be good? Ain't nobody gonna pick you cause you'd be *good.* These here are farm folks. They're looking for somebody that can milk cows or drive a tractor. Ain't that right, Jim?" Frank poked his elbow in his friend's ribs.

Jim mumbled around a mouthful of mashed potatoes. "Thas right. Need to be strong."

I used my spoon to make a bigger crater for the lava butter. "I'm strong. I could learn to milk a cow," I muttered toward my potato mountain.

Frank tipped on his chair as he laughed. He pointed across the table with his fork. "You're a scrawny little boy. Ain't no way you can work on a farm." He laughed again and elbowed Jim who sputtered a little around his potatoes.

My spoon caved in the crater, then chopped the mountain into pieces that ran together. I longed for something to say that would make Frank stop talking. Maybe if I just ignored him. I spooned some of the potatoes in my mouth.

Ignoring didn't work. Frank just rattled on. "I'm gonna get someone that wants me to drive the tractor. I already know how cause I drove my Uncle Ted's car once."

Frank was right. I didn't know anything about farms. And while I didn't exactly think of myself as scrawny, I was the smallest of all the boys who came to Iowa.

Although he'd refilled and eaten everything on his plate twice, Frank didn't stop talking. "Course, some of the people are just looking for a kid. You know, they don't have one, so they take in an orphan. Your sister'll be one of those. She's little enough. Someone'll take her to be their kid."

My spoon clattered to my plate, and my stomach clenched. "They won't take her without me. We go together."

Frank's laughter sent a chunk of chicken from his mouth flying across the table. It landed on the white tablecloth near my arm. As his laughter subsided, Frank's elbow nudged Jim again. "Hear that? Sissy Boy thinks he'll get to go with his sister." He swept his hand in the direction of Emma's table. "She's little. She'll be one of the first to go, but you're probably going to have a long ride back to New York. Ain't nobody gonna want you."

The knot in my stomach grew until there was room for nothing but fear. Not the chicken thigh with only one bite taken. Not the half-eaten potato mountain. Not the coleslaw. I sipped from my glass of milk, but even it tasted sour. When I looked over at Emma, she was laughing, her eyes sparkling and dimple showing. Mrs. Johnson smiled down at her and one hand reached out and touched Emma's cheek, perhaps wiping off a bit of food.

I sat miserably, waiting for Mr. Carter to tell us to line up for the opera house. That was the place where someone could take my sister away from me.

CHAPTER 4

The line of children snaked around the dining room behind Mr. Carter and Mrs. Johnson. Emma waved to those at her table before scooting over to hold tight to my hand. "Are we going to the opera house? Are we going to meet our family? Do I look pretty?"

Instead of answering, I squeezed her hand. "Shh. Mr. Carter's talking."

She wouldn't stand still. She hopped from one foot to the other, wiggled so her skirt flopped against my legs, and then jumped. I jerked her arm so she would stay in the line and listen to Mr. Carter.

"Ow!" she yelped.

All eyes turned in our direction. Mr. Carter glared at us, and Emma stood frozen by my side.

"Is there a problem?" Mr. Carter asked in an icy tone.

"No, sir." Now I did the glaring at my sister.

Mr. Carter swiveled, and the line marched out of the hotel and toward the opera house. I hadn't heard a word of his directions to us.

Outside the wooden sidewalk was full of people, and they all seemed to be going to the opera house. As we passed by groups of people or they passed us, I could hear the whispers and comments. I wished the iron horse would roll by so I could hop on and go back to New York.

We entered the opera house by a side door. Mrs. Johnson used a key to unlock it, and we all scrunched into a tiny room. Emma clutched my leg, and my face was inches away from Ruth's back. I hoped I wouldn't throw up.

Mrs. Johnson gave us a huge smile. "In a few minutes, children, you can follow me onto the stage and sit in one of the chairs. Mr. Carter will tell a little bit about each of you. Prospective guardians will be making application to take some of you home tonight. Of course, there may be children who stay at the Mason Hotel for a few more nights until a suitable guardian is found."

And those of us that nobody chose would return to New York.

The mass of bodies surged forward. I gripped Emma's hand tightly. Two wooden steps led to the stage. I walked up and saw what must have been hundreds of eyes staring back at me. Emma let go of my hand and slid into a chair next to Ruth. She smoothed down the skirt of her dress like a real lady, like Mama would have. I swallowed the lump in my throat and walked to the last empty chair way at the end of the line beside Frank. I slumped into the chair and tried to pretend I was sitting on a stairway in a New York alley and that all those eyes belonged to people passing by, not even looking at me.

As soon as the first child stepped on the stage, a hum of whispered voices rose from the crowd and rolled toward us like a wave. After we were seated and Mrs. Johnson and Mr. Carter stepped forward, it went out like the tide.

Mrs. Johnson beamed out at the crowd. Maybe she smiled all the time. "Welcome, friends and neighbors of the Oak Hill community"

I didn't listen to what she said next. She droned on for several minutes, then Mr. Carter stepped forward and stood by Ruth. "This is Ruth Harrison. She's a strong, healthy child with a pleasant disposition." My mind skittered away. What could Mr. Carter say about me?

Ruth stood up and began reciting a lengthy poem. I'd forgotten about this. We'd all been required to learn a poem or Bible verse before we left. When she was finished, she sat down, and there was a polite spattering of applause.

When Mr. Carter stepped over to Emma and put his hand on her head, the murmuring wave began again. Every eye in the house was fastened on my sister. "Isn't this a sweet little lady? Just look at those sparkling eyes. She's healthy as can be and a very intelligent child."

Emma's eyes were wide and frightened. She looked at me, and I gave her a little smile.

"Now Emma will give a recitation."

Emma stood, one hand twisting a piece of her hair. I knew her poem by heart for we'd worked at it together. Her voice trembled as she spoke.

The ginger-jar stood snugly hid,
And this is what the Baby did:
He climbed to where the dainties are,
And, reaching for that hidden jar,
He thrust his naughty fingers in it!
But he repented it next minute.
A little mouse had just then come;
He thought it was a sweetmeat crumb—
And fell to nibbling Baby's thumb:
    Tweak! squeak!
    Shriek! shriek!

The opera house erupted with laughter. The applause lasted a long while. Emma sat down and gave a nervous little smile.

When the audience finally quieted down, Mr. Carter moved to the next child. Slowly, as the clock ticked on, he crept down the line toward me. Maybe it would be so late he'd just skip me. I rehearsed my lines in my head. The Beatitudes. I could do it.

". . . strong as a young horse. This young man will be a great help on any farm." Mr. Carter patted Frank's shoulder. Then Frank stood and mumbled a poem about a battle. I couldn't hear it over the pounding of my heart.

Mr. Carter stood behind me. "This is Bert Davidson. His mother died and his father surrendered him to the Children's Aid Society a few months ago. Emma Davidson is his sister." He nodded toward Emma's chair, and she squirmed and smiled at me. "He may not be as big as some of our older boys, but he is healthy and a willing worker. I am sure you would find him a great help on a farm."

His hand on my shoulder gave a little nudge, and I knew I was supposed to get up and recite, but my mind went blank. Totally blank. I rose, and my legs quivered like the red Jell-O that Shirley served for dessert one night.

"The Beatitudes." My voice squeaked. I cleared my throat and tried again. "The Beatitudes." Nothing. I couldn't remember anything. "Blessed are the . . ." I looked at Mr. Carter for help. He scowled, his face a bright red.

I shook my head. There was no applause when I plunked down in my chair. I wanted to sink through the floor of the stage.

Mr. Carter's hand grasped my shoulder. "Well, don't let this deter you from giving a home to the boy."

Mrs. Johnson gave me a little half smile before she turned to the audience. "The committee and I will be set up in the lobby. Come and fill out an application so you

can take one of these children home tonight. For those of you who have already completed the forms, we are in the process of matching children to families. Please enjoy the refreshments provided by the members of our committee."

She stepped down from the stage and hurried through the crowd toward the lobby.

Mr. Carter looked at me in disgust and shook his head. "I'm not sure we'll find anyone to take you now. They all think you're dimwitted." He raised his head and spoke to all the children. "Remain seated until someone calls your name." Then he walked down and began shaking hands and talking to some of the people.

I could see a line forming in the lobby in front of the table where Mrs. Johnson and the other committee members sat. I tried to sit still, but my legs ached to get up and run. On the other side of Fred, blond-haired Sarah, the only girl younger than Emma, had fallen asleep in her chair. Her head lolled to one side.

"Sarah O'Leary." One of the women I recognized as being on the committee stood at the edge of the stage. She had a wide smile on her face. A man and woman stood close behind her.

Ruth stood, moved to Sarah's chair, and patted the little girl's back. "Sarah, honey, wake up. I think you have a new home." The man lifted her into his arms, and the woman spread her arms around both of them so they formed a circle.

As they left the stage, Sarah raised her head from her new dad's shoulder. She blinked sleepy eyes, but then she smiled and waved.

Next one of the boys was picked. He giggled as he walked hand in hand with his family. He didn't look back.

Another couple started down the aisle. I knew as soon as I saw them. They'd come for Emma. The man looked important like the men that walked the streets of New York with suit coats and hats and newspapers tucked under their arms. His wife wore a silky blue dress with dots all over, kinda like someone had splashed something, but it splashed in perfectly round, even dots. Her hair was piled up on her head like Mama used to wear hers. Maybe she even looked like Mama, a little. Mrs. Johnson was with them, and she talked to the woman all the way to the stage.

Mrs. Johnson looked at my sister and smiled. "Emma Davidson."

Emma bounced from her chair. "I'm Emma."

The four of them stood talking for a few minutes. Emma pointed at me, and the man shook his head. The woman took Emma's hand, and they started off the stage.

Suddenly Emma tugged free, whirled around, and raced across the stage. She clung to me, and I could feel her heart beating. "No, Bert. I won't go without you. Don't let them take me away."

I peeled her arms off my neck. Swallowing hard, I whispered to her. "You must, Emma. This is why we came to Iowa."

Tears formed in her blue eyes and spilled down her cheeks. "Oh, Bert, I don't want to leave you. When will I see you again? Will you come visit me in my new home?"

"Sure, I will."

"Promise?"

"Pinky promise." I held out my finger, and she linked her little pinky in mine. Then I hugged her tight.

She swiped a hand across her eyes and sniffled. Then she walked slowly across the stage and took hold of her new parents' hands again.

This must be what a broken heart felt like. And how could I ever keep my promise?

CHAPTER 5

The long night wore on, and one by one the others left. A huge bear of a man dressed in jeans approached the stage, followed by a woman with a bright smile. I thought he was looking in my direction, but Mrs. Johnson called out, "Frank Pearson."

Frank didn't wait for them to come on the stage. He vaulted down and stuck out his hand. Then he threw a triumphant look at me over his shoulder. I sat on the stage by myself. Most of the townspeople were gone now. In the lobby the committee members stood and gathered up papers.

Mr. Carter appeared suddenly beside me. "Come on, Bert. We'll stay the night in the hotel. There are more applications and people to contact tomorrow. The committee still thinks they can get you placed."

I followed him to the hotel. He didn't talk to me, and that was okay. My mind churned with my own thoughts. Mostly about Emma and her new home. Would they be good to her? Would they feed her fruit? She loved apples. Would she sing her funny little songs to them?

At the hotel there was a cot made up for me in Mr. Carter's room. It wasn't much different from the bed I'd had at the orphanage. I washed up, lay down, and pulled the blanket up to my chin. Would Mr. Carter ride the train with me when we went back to New York? Or would they ship me in a box like an unwanted parcel?

When I woke, Mr. Carter's snoring reverberated through the room. I peeked through my eyelashes. He lay on his back, his hands clasped across his middle, his mouth gaping open. I needed to use the toilet, but I didn't want to wake him. I turned on my side, then on my back, but I still needed to go. Finally I eased off the cot and trotted to the bathroom. When I flushed the toilet, it sounded like a waterfall. And when I returned to the room, Mr. Carter was sitting up, rubbing his eyes.

I perched on the edge of my cot, being careful not to tip it. "Good morning, Mr. Carter."

"Good morning, Bert." His voice didn't sound like he really wanted any conversation, so I went to the window, pushed the curtain to the side, and looked out.

The morning sun shone down on Oak Hill. A few men and women strode down the sidewalk, looking as if they knew where they were going and what they needed to do. I could see the edge of the train depot building in the distance. Suddenly the day didn't seem so bright.

I took my folded clothes off the chair and put them on, trying to smooth out the wrinkles in my new shirt.

Mr. Carter emerged from the bathroom. His hair was wet and shiny, combed back, and he wore a clean white shirt. He looked at his pocket watch lying on the dresser. "We meet with Mrs. Johnson in the lobby in an hour. Let's go have some breakfast."

The dining room looked larger than it did yesterday when all the chairs held kids. Mr. Carter chose a table near the window. He ordered for both of us, a bowl of oatmeal for me and eggs, biscuits, and sausage gravy for him. He unfolded a newspaper he'd picked up in the lobby and began to read as he ate.

I tried to read the other side of the paper, but Mr. Carter kept moving it, so I gave up and watched out the window.

After what seemed like a very long time, the paper dropped to the table. "It's time to go," Mr. Carter announced. He stood, folded the paper, and tucked it under his arm.

Just as we entered the lobby, Mrs. Johnson sped through the heavy glass door as if it had plucked her off the sidewalk and pushed her inside. She smiled when she saw us.

"Good news, Bert. I went through the applications one more time, and I think I've found a family willing to take you in. The Vogels own a farm about five miles south of town. They had filled out an application but were unable to come to the opera house last night. I visited them this morning, and they want to meet you." She paused, a little breathless, as if she'd run to get here.

"When?" My voice squeaked out.

"Right now." She turned to Mr. Carter. "I have my car waiting outside, if you're ready."

My stomach flip-flopped. Not only was I going to a farm to meet my new family, I would have my first-ever ride in an automobile. New York streets were filled with them. They went speeding around the frightened horses, splashing mud on unsuspecting pedestrians, and carrying important-looking passengers. But I'd never had anyone offer to take me for a ride.

I rocked on my heels a little until Mr. Carter looked at me and frowned.

"Wait one moment, please." Mr. Carter stepped to the desk and spoke with the mustached man behind it, then returned. We followed Mrs. Johnson outside.

A shiny, black Ford waited in front. A well-dressed young man sat with one hand on the steering wheel and the other draped casually out the window.

Mrs. Johnson patted the man's arm with a white-gloved hand. "This is my son, Theodore. He works with his father at the bank, but this morning he offered to drive me out to the Vogels'."

Mr. Carter shook his hand, and I said, "Hello, sir." Then Mr. Carter opened the door to the back seat, and, after he motioned with his hand, I scooted in. The car was all black inside with different kinds of instruments and gauges across the dashboard. The seats were padded, smooth, and soft. I inhaled the odor, a mixture of gasoline, oil, and leather.

Theodore turned a key, and the engine roared to life. He pushed on a pedal, moved the gear shift, and we jerked forward. I clutched the edge of the seat and peered out the open window. We sped up until it seemed we were flying down Main Street. I looked over Theodore's shoulder at the speedometer. Twenty-five miles an hour!

Outside of town the car slowed as we turned onto a rutted one-lane road. Fields stretched on either side. Some of them had been plowed and looked as thick and rich as a slab of Shirley's chocolate cake. Some still held the remnants of last year's corn harvest, dry and brown stalks that waved brittle leaves as we passed.

We turned into an even narrower driveway. A faded red barn towered above a white two-story house. My heart hammered so loud I was sure they could hear it over the sound of the car's motor.

Theodore stopped the car, and I almost slid off the seat. A thin man came out of the barn, wiped his hands on his overalls, and walked toward us. A screen door banged and a woman stepped out onto the porch. She wore a dress with an apron tied over it.

Mr. Carter and Mrs. Johnson got out of the car. Mrs. Johnson opened the door on my side. "Come on. They won't bite."

I'd never felt so unsure of myself. Pa used to tell me, "Hold your head up and people think you belong." So I tipped my chin up, but I couldn't make my mouth smile.

The woman came to stand beside the man in overalls. Mrs. Johnson took hold of my arm, and we walked toward them.

"Good morning, Mr. and Mrs. Vogel. This is Bert, the boy I told you about." Mrs. Johnson gave me a little nudge, so I stuck out my hand.

Mr. Vogel shook my hand and looked me over from head to toe. "He's not very big."

Mrs. Johnson's smile never dimmed. "No, but he'll grow, and he's healthy."

Mrs. Vogel scowled. "Growing means he'll eat a lot."

I couldn't keep my chin up any longer. I watched the toe of one shoe scuff up the dust. "I may not be big, but I'm strong. I'll work hard for you, mister."

Mrs. Vogel shook her finger as if she were scolding me. "There's no time for playing on a farm. You'd have to get chores done before you go to school, then help again when you get home."

I nodded, a little hope rising in my heart. "I can do that."

Mr. Carter spoke up. "He's a good boy. He won't disappoint you." I looked at him in surprise. I'd never heard him compliment me before. Maybe he just didn't want me tagging along on the long ride back to New York.

Mr. Vogel spoke up. "Give me and the missus a minute."

Mrs. Johnson nodded. "Certainly."

The Vogels turned their backs to us. I could hear them whispering. "He looks . . . taking a chance . . . won't be the same . . ."

I wished there was a magic formula I could chant or a prayer I could say, but I gave up praying when Mama died.

Mr. Vogel turned back to face us. "We'll give it a try. If it doesn't work out, we can contact you?"

Mr. Carter responded. "Of course. I'll visit Monday, so we can finalize the contract. You can change your mind before then. And after that, we keep in contact by mail. If this doesn't work out for either of you," he paused and looked first at me, then at the Vogels, "we'll send someone to pick Bert up."

I had a home. A home in Oak Hill, Iowa. I was going to be the best farmer's helper I could be.

CHAPTER 6

Theodore turned the car around, and with a little spurt of dirt from the wheels he drove off down the lane. I watched as they disappeared in a rolling cloud of dust.

Mrs. Vogel pointed at the paper sack I clutched in my hand. "That all you got?"

I nodded. "It's my extra socks and shirt." I had a pair of underwear in there too, but I didn't want to say that out loud.

"Those don't look much like work clothes. Come in the house. I have some things that may fit you."

I followed her into the house, letting the screen door bang behind me.

Mrs. Vogel spoke without turning. "Don't let the door slam."

I hung my head. "Yes, ma'am. I won't do it again."

"You can sit there and wait for me." She motioned to a high-backed wooden chair at the kitchen table, then she walked around the corner and up a narrow flight of stairs.

I pulled a chair out and looked around. The large kitchen was clean and bright. Two pies sat cooling on a rack on the counter. My mouth watered, and I hoped we'd get a piece for lunch. Through the doorway I could see what looked like a living room with a couch and an overstuffed chair. Beside the chair was a tall shelf filled with books. I didn't know anyone could own that many books. I wanted to take them off the shelf and see if they had pictures, but I thought I'd better stay put.

After a long time I heard Mrs. Vogel's footsteps on the stairs. I sat up straighter. She carried a pile of clothes, which she handed to me. "I think these will fit you. You're kind of scrawny for ten. I'll show you where you can change."

I followed her back upstairs where she motioned to a closed door. "You can dress in there. You'll sleep there tonight."

I nodded and opened the door. A narrow bed with a metal headboard backed against one wall. A tall wooden dresser stood against the opposite wall. I peeked out the window. I could see for miles. The fields stretched out in every direction, one of them divided by a line of trees. Far in the distance I could see tracks and a train like the one that had brought me to Iowa.

I spread the clothes out on the crazy quilt that covered the bed. There were two pairs of patched overalls, two faded shirts, some socks, underwear, and pajamas. Who did the clothes belong to?

I stripped out of my clothes, folded them, and laid them on the bed. Then I slipped into one of the shirts and overalls Mrs. Vogel had given me. They fit as if they'd been made for me. I hurried downstairs.

Mrs. Vogel waited for me in the kitchen. Her eyes took in my clothes. Then she blinked hard, like she had something in her eyes. She turned away abruptly. "Let's go find Mr. Vogel and see what he wants you to do this morning."

We stepped out on the porch, where she cupped her hands to her mouth and called. "Roy . . . Roy."

I don't know why I was surprised. Everybody has a first name. I just didn't know that Mr. Vogel did. Within a few moments he stepped out of the barn and walked toward us. When he saw me in the overalls, he stared at Mrs. Vogel.

"The boy needed some work clothes," she said softly.

Mr. Vogel frowned, then he nodded at her before turning to me. "Ready to get to work?"

"Yep." I stuck my hands in the deep pockets of my overalls.

"Ever been in a chicken house?"

"No, sir." I'd never been up close to a chicken, unless you counted those that were fried and on a plate.

"Follow me." Mr. Vogel walked toward a small building with a low slanted roof and a fence surrounding it. He opened a gate in the fence, and after I stepped in, he latched it behind us. He opened the little door in the building and suddenly fat birds rushed through in a burst of feathers and cackling. I shrieked and covered my head.

"You scared of these little ole chickens, boy?" Mr. Vogel sounded amused.

I dropped my hands to my side, feeling my face grow warm. "They just surprised me. That's all."

Mr. Vogel ducked his head as he went inside the building. I followed. The smell inside was horrible, worse than the gutters in New York. The walls were lined with boxes stuffed with straw. Mr. Vogel picked up a round bushel basket and hauled it over next to the boxes. "Take all the dirty bedding out of the nests and put it in the bushel basket. We got a manure spreader back of the barn you can dump it in. Then I'll show you where to get fresh straw." He stepped back out of the door.

I put my hand in the first box and touched something wet and gooey. Holding my nose with my other hand, I scooped the soggy, soiled straw out. Then I moved to the next box. After about the third box, I gave up holding my nose. I could work more efficiently if I used both hands. When the bushel basket was full, I backed out of the hen house, dragging the dirty bedding. The hens cackled and fluttered about me. I dragged the basket to the wire fence, maneuvered it through, and latched the gate behind me.

I knew I was to empty the basket into a manure spreader, but where was it? And what was it? Mr. Vogel had said behind the barn. I made my way slowly in that direction. The basket bounced and scraped along behind me. When I rounded the corner of the barn, I saw a wagon. It had a mound of soiled straw with a pitchfork sticking out of the middle like a flagpole.

The rear of the wagon, with a wheel-like contraption attached, was backed up to an open door into the barn. The wooden sides towered above me. This must be the spreader. I looked down at that smelly mess in the bushel basket and then up where I was to put it.

Using both hands, I lifted it. When it reached chest level, I rested it against the wagon. Then getting under the basket, I pushed it up. Suddenly the basket tipped. But not into the wagon as I'd planned. It tipped over me, spilling all that smelly, gooey straw over my head, my arms, and the clean clothes Mrs. Vogel had given me.

As I scrambled to get away from it, my foot slipped on the wet straw, and I plunked down, manure raining down around me. The big basket struck my head on its way to the ground, rolling a little before stopping.

I sat in that mess and wanted to cry like Emma.

"What's going on here?" Mr. Vogel strode around the corner of the barn.

"I was trying to empty the basket." I hated it when my voice quivered. "I spilled it." I spit out a piece of straw and wondered if he'd hit me or just holler a little.

"Well, we better get this cleaned up, and then I'll show you where the pump is so you can clean up too." Mr. Vogel reached up in the wagon, pulled down the pitch fork, and handed it to me.

I scraped the soggy bits of straw off the ground and back in the basket as best I could. When I'd gotten most of it in, Mr. Vogel swung the basket up and upended it into the wagon.

He set the basket down and turned to me. "Don't ever be afraid to ask for help when you need it."

A bell rang. It sounded like the one used to call us in from play at the orphanage.

"Missus has lunch ready for us. I'll show you where the pump is." Mr. Vogel poked the pitch fork back into the mound of manure, then he walked toward the house.

The pump stood in the side yard and a small basin, towel, and thick bar of yellow soap lay on a bench beside it. Mr. Vogel moved the handle up and down until a steady stream of water appeared. I ducked my head under it. The water was cold, and I shivered as it ran down my neck and under the thin shirt. I rubbed the foul-smelling goop out of my hair.

Mr. Vogel handed me the bar of soap, and I scrubbed at my face, hands, and arms. Most of the manure and straw was gone, but my clothes were soaked. I used the towel to wipe off as best I could. Mr. Vogel used the soap and washed his hands too, then I followed him into the kitchen. It seemed a long time ago since I'd had the bowl of oatmeal in Oak Hill. The smells inside made my stomach growl.

Mrs. Vogel turned from the stove where she was stirring a pot of something. "Boy, you're soaked. You only need to wash your hands for lunch, not your whole body."

"Sorry." I mumbled. Mr. Vogel didn't tell her the whole embarrassing story, so I wasn't going to tell her either.

"Little problem mucking out the henhouse." Mr. Vogel sat in one of the chairs at the table. "Sit down, boy."

I slid into a chair as Mrs. Vogel carried a steaming platter of meat and potatoes. I reached for one of the thick slices of bread already on the table.

"We say grace before we eat at this house." Mrs. Vogel said as she set the platter down.

"Sorry," I said for the second time since I'd come in the kitchen, then I bowed my head.

Mr. Vogel spoke the prayer. "Almighty God, we thank you for this food and the hands that have prepared it. Bless the food to its intended use. And thanks for this boy. In the name of our Savior, Jesus Christ, we pray. Amen."

I looked up in astonishment. No one, ever, had thanked God for me before.

CHAPTER 7

After lunch, we had a rest time. Mr. Vogel sat in a chair in the front room, tipped his head back, and started snoring. Mrs. Vogel sewed on some material in her lap. Every other stitch she would glance up at me as if to make sure I was still there, but she never smiled.

The next thing I knew, Mr. Vogel shook my shoulder. "Time to go to work, boy."

I stumbled to my feet. My shirt had dried, but my pants were still a little damp and smelly.

Outside Mr. Vogel showed me the clean straw in the barn. I finished cleaning out the nests, then stuffed them with clean straw and put the bushel basket away. We cleaned out the stalls where the horses and cow went in the barn.

Later I helped him feed the cow, the sow and her eight little piglets, and the chickens. I stood and watched as he milked the cow.

"Watch what I'm doing. This'll be your job when I start planting." Mr. Vogel spoke with his head resting on the cow's soft side. I watched as he reached under the cow and squeezed out the milk. I looked at her wide hips and big pointy hooves, and I hoped it would be a long time until planting.

We washed up again before going inside. Supper was leftovers from dinner warmed up, but they tasted even better the second time, especially the peach pie.

After supper Mr. Vogel brought a large round galvanized tub in from the porch and set it in the middle of the kitchen floor. Mrs. Vogel poured a large pot of steaming water into it that she'd heated on the stove and then added cool water until it was half full. She handed me another bar of the yellow soap, a worn towel, and the pair of pajamas that had been on my bed. "Scrub everywhere. Can't have you smelling at church tomorrow. And just leave those dirty clothes there. I'll wash them Monday."

I began slowly unbuttoning my shirt. Was she going to watch me take a bath?

"I'll be in the front room if you need something." Mrs. Vogel left.

When I climbed into the tub, the water rose. I sank down and let the warm water slosh around me. Every muscle in my body ached. At the orphanage we had plenty of chores, but I'd never worked as hard as I had today.

Using the bar of soap I scrubbed everywhere like she'd said. Then I did it a second time just to make sure. I splashed water over me to rinse off. Some water sloshed over the side of the tub. Then when I stood and reached for the towel, I dripped more water on the floor. I dried quickly and slipped the pajamas on. They were striped and soft.

I hung the towel over the back of the chair and stepped into the front room. Mr. Vogel had a book in his lap. He didn't look up. Mrs. Vogel looked over her glasses at me. "Did you scrub?"

"Yes, ma'am." I nodded, sprinkling water from my wet hair onto my shoulders.

"Is the floor wet?"

I hesitated. I really didn't like getting into trouble, but usually a lie meant more trouble than the truth. "I think I kinda dripped some."

She bit a thread in two and began to knot it. "Go clean it up."

I went back in the kitchen, took down my damp towel, and sopped up the water on the floor. When I finished, she was standing behind me, her sewing draped over one arm.

"Good night, boy." She held out a small kerosene lantern. "There's some books on the shelf in your bedroom. You can read them if you wish, but there will be chores to do before church tomorrow, so don't stay up too late. And don't forget to blow out the lamp."

"Okay. Good night." I started up the narrow stairs to the room where I'd changed clothes earlier.

The lantern cast shadows on the walls. When I stepped into the bedroom, the light spread a warm glow over the room. A wooden shelf stood beside the bed. It held at least ten books neatly in a row. A wooden puzzle, an Uncle Wiggly game, and a crude wooden carving of a dog perched on the bottom shelf.

I pulled a book with a dark blue cover off the shelf. *The Adventures of Tom Sawyer.* On the first page, there was a picture of a house not too different from the one I was in and a boy not too different from me. I sat on the bed and started reading.

"Tom!"

No answer.

"You!"

No answer.

I'd read only a few pages before my eyes got all droopy. I put the book back on the shelf, blew out the lantern, then peeled back the crazy quilt and slid between the sheets. I scrunched down until my head sank onto the pillow.

I wondered if somewhere, tucked under another quilt, Emma said the prayer I'd taught her.

It felt like I'd been asleep only a short time when I heard Mr. Vogel's voice. "Boy! You gonna sleep all day? That cow out there needs milking. Come on."

I rolled out from under the quilt. The floor was cold, and I grabbed the second set of overalls and shirt and jammed my legs and arms in the right places. Through the window the pale dawn light made a faint square on the floor. I pulled on socks, but I carried my shoes downstairs.

In the kitchen, Mr. Vogel had lit the kerosene lamp in the center of the table. "You drink coffee?" he asked me.

"No, sir. At least I've never had any."

"Probably a good thing. Might stunt your growth, and you aren't much to begin with."

I pulled on my shoes and laced them tightly. When I finished tying them, Mr. Vogel set his cup on the table. "Ready to milk?"

I thought about how big the cow was and imagined reaching underneath and pulling her . . . what did he call them? "I can try." I gulped down fear.

Mr. Vogel lifted a clean bucket from the counter and stepped out on the porch. I followed, being careful not to let the screen door slam. When he opened the barn door, there was a gentle moo and the soft thump of animal feet. From the feed bin he scooped up a small bucket of shelled corn. He poured this into a trough, and the cow stuck her head through an opening between two wooden bars. Mr. Vogel slid one of the bars over, so she couldn't back out. The cow didn't seem to mind. She reached down for a mouthful of corn and chewed contentedly.

"Does she have a name?" I asked, following Mr. Vogel through a door into the cow's stall.

"Bossy. I call her Bossy." He ran his hand along her back and patted her flank. "Get the stool, boy."

I hurried to lift the one-legged stool from its place on the wall. How would I ever balance on this and get the milk in the bucket?

"Let her know you're there." Mr. Vogel directed.

I gave her a gentle pat. "Hi, Bossy. I'm Bert."

"Now sit on the stool." He motioned and stepped back.

I positioned the stool next to the cow's large belly and squatted down until I was sitting.

Mr. Vogel handed me the bucket. "Put this between your knees."

After the bucket was in place, he continued. "Now wrap your hand around the teat and gently squeeze and pull down."

I reached out and grasped the udder. When I squeezed two or three little drops of milk spattered like raindrops into the bucket. I tried again and a tiny stream of milk hit the metal with a tinkling sound. I kept pulling and soon I had about a cup of milk in the bucket. At that moment Bossy's tail swung around and hit me on the side of my face. I leaned back and the stool tipped, spilling me and the bucket of milk into the straw bedding.

Mr. Vogel grabbed the bucket and my arm at the same time, lifting me to my feet. "Her tail isn't gonna hurt you. Now sit back down and try it again."

I wanted to protest, to say I couldn't do it, but that didn't seem like an option. I repositioned the stool, the bucket, and myself and tried again. When I'd doubled what I had in the bucket before Bossy slapped me with her tail, Mr. Vogel took over.

"Watch how I do it," he said. In a very short time, he'd filled the bucket.

He handed it to me. "Take it in to the missus, then I'll show you how to get the eggs and feed those hens."

By the time we'd finished and washed up at the pump, I felt like we'd put in an entire day's worth of work.

Mrs. Vogel had plates of bacon, eggs, and toast for all of us and a glass of creamy milk for me. I'd spent the morning getting milk and eggs, and now I was eating them.

"Please pass the strawberry jam." I layered the sweet syrupy spread on my toast and took a big bite. Then I washed it down with milk.

Mrs. Vogel stood and carried her dishes to the sink. "As soon as you're finished eating, get dressed for church. I laid out your clothes on the bed. Don't dilly-dally now. We don't want to be late."

I swallowed the last bite of the eggs, drained my milk, and carried my empty plate to her.

"Go." Mrs. Vogel made a shooing motion with her hand. "I'll take care of the dishes this time."

I scooted upstairs and put on the pants and shirt lying on the bed. The pants were a little short, but the shirt fit. I used a brush I spotted on the dresser to smooth my hair. When I looked out the window, I could see Mr. Vogel sitting on the seat of a wagon behind one of the sturdy horses I'd help feed yesterday. He'd changed to a shirt and pants, and he even wore a nice hat.

I clattered down the stairs. Mrs. Vogel appeared from nowhere and scowled. "We don't run in the house."

I skidded to a stop. "Sorry. I saw Mr. Vogel outside."

"He won't leave without us." She draped a black shawl around her shoulders, picked up her purse, and marched out the door.

I followed, making sure I walked. Mrs. Vogel climbed up onto the seat beside her husband, and I scrambled in back. Mr. Vogel made a clucking noise, and the horse started off. I clutched the side of the wagon, trying to keep from bouncing around as the wagon wheels hit every bump in the road.

The church was on a hilltop not too far from the Vogel farm. I could hear a piano playing as the wagon turned in. Mr. Vogel tied the horse to a hitching rack, and we all three went inside. When I saw Frank sitting between the large man and thin woman, relief flooded over me. Someone I knew. I raised my hand in a little wave. He nodded at me and smiled, but Mrs. Vogel pushed my hand down.

We stopped in front of an empty pew, and Mr. Vogel motioned for me to sit. I slid on the polished wood surface to make room for Mrs. Vogel and him. Then someone said, "Hymn number one-thirty-nine, 'Bringing in the Sheaves.'"

Mrs. Vogel leafed through the pages, then held the hymnbook so I could read the words. I hadn't been in a church since my mom took us when Emma was a baby. I tried to sing the unfamiliar words.

When the song ended, several people talked. They made announcements, took an offering, and then gave a long sermon about, of all things, the Beatitudes. I really didn't want to hear that. The preacher called them "a blueprint for living." One by one he went through each of the Beatitudes. God wanted us to be poor in spirit, merciful, meek, pure in heart, hungry and thirsty for righteousness, and peacemakers.

That was way too much to take in. I wasn't sure I could be any of those things.

When the service was over, I trailed behind the Vogels to the door. Mrs. Vogel kept stopping to talk to someone. A plump gray-haired lady in a flower-laden hat peered around Mrs. Vogel at me and smiled. "And who might this handsome lad be?"

Mrs. Vogel looked back as if she were surprised to find me behind her. "This is our boy from New York. He came on the orphan train."

I felt like everyone in the whole church stopped talking to stare at me. For the first time in my life, I wished I were smaller . . . small enough to crawl under the pews and get away.

"What a handsome young man. Do you have a name?" The lady's eyes were kind and made me not wish quite so much to crawl away.

"I'm Bert Davidson, ma'am."

"And what nice manners. I bet you're a big help to Mr. and Mrs. Vogel. And a great comfort too." She patted my head like I was a puppy.

"Thank you. I'm not so much help yet. I keep spilling things."

The lady burst into laughter, the flowers on her hat shaking like they were in a wind storm.

"I'll see you Tuesday afternoon at Missionary Circle," Mrs. Vogel said as she propelled me toward the door.

A line formed at the door where the pastor stood and greeted everyone. I didn't look forward to another explanation of how I came to Iowa. Through the open door I could see Mr. Vogel at the wagon.

"Can I go outside with Mr. Vogel? Please?"

Mrs. Vogel looked at me in surprise. "I guess so."

Weaving through the knot of people at the door, I slipped out and jogged down the steps. When I reached the wagon, Mr. Vogel was sitting on the seat.

"Hop in back, boy," he said without looking.

CHAPTER 8

"Another piece of chicken?" Mrs. Vogel held out the platter.

"No thanks." I shook my head. It was the best fried chicken I'd ever had. But after eating two legs, two biscuits, mashed potatoes and gravy, and green beans, I felt like I was going to burst.

"Well, at least we'll get some meat on your bones." Mrs. Vogel offered the platter to her husband, but he shook his head.

When he rose, I did too. "What are we doing this afternoon?"

Mrs. Vogel waved a dirty fork. "This is the Lord's day. We never work."

"You help the missus with the dishes and then you'll have some free time." Mr. Vogel headed into the front room.

I dried the dishes while Mrs. Vogel washed them. When she hung up the towel and her apron, I knew we were through. "Can I go outside to play?"

Mrs. Vogel seemed to consider my request for a moment before granting it. "I guess so. Just stay out of trouble."

I walked out on the porch. If Emma were here, she'd be wanting me to play house or something. But I was Robin Hood, leading my merry men, just like the characters in the book Mama read.

A branch under the maple tree made a nifty sword. I ran through the yard, brandishing the sword at my enemies and rescuing princesses. If Emma were here, she could be a princess.

I headed to the barn, dragging my sword behind me. Every good knight needs a steed. The two big black horses stood under a tree in the barnyard. Mr. Vogel called them Edith and Forest. I opened the gate and walked toward them. Their ears perked forward, and they watched me. They were enormous and probably had enormous teeth too.

I turned around and went in the barn. In the center of the barn was a ladder with rungs that led upward to an opening into the second story. A hay loft. I climbed up, clutching my sword under one arm. It was dark in the loft with little bits of light filtering through the cracks. I could hear rustling, and I grasped the stick, wishing it was a real sword.

A tiger-striped kitten emerged from between two bales of hay.

"You're not much of an enemy." I put down my sword and sat in the piles of loose hay. The kitten ambled over and climbed in my lap, purring and rubbing her head against my arm. I petted her until she hopped off and walked away, probably in search of a mouse meal.

My eyes had adjusted to the darkness, so I climbed on the hay. I thrust my sword into the crevices, killing the dragons that lurked in the great mountains and cliffs.

Then I slid and bumped my way down. When my legs and arms grew itchy from the hay, I picked up my sword and climbed down the ladder.

Bossy was in her stall, peering through the stanchion at me with her chocolate-brown eyes.

"Is it almost milking time, girl?" I eyed her feedbox. If I stood on it, I might be able to swing up on her back. "Would you like to be a knight's steed?" I gave her golden back a pat, and she didn't move. I clambered up on the feedbox. She watched me, but she still didn't move. I put one leg over her back and hoisted myself up. But as she turned to look, my sword whacked her in the nose. With a snort she tossed her head, whirled and galloped out of the barn, and the knight and his sword landed on the barn floor.

"What's going on in here?" Mr. Vogel walked in the side door.

"Um, Bossy got scared of something."

He looked at me sitting on the floor, then outside at Bossy who had retreated a distance away from the barn. "And what would that be?"

I wished I could crawl back into the haymow and hide. "Me. I thought maybe she'd like to give me a ride on her back."

Mr. Vogel slammed open the gate into Bossy's stall. "Boy, don't you know, you don't scare the cow? She won't let her milk down if she's frightened. Go on now. Get the chickens in, and try not to spill anything."

I edged out the door and hurried to the henhouse. I hadn't actually spilled anything but me this time. I rubbed my sore backside. And I'd left my sword in Bossy's stall.

That night after we had leftover chicken and biscuits, Mr. Vogel read to us from the big Bible in the front room. As he closed the book, he looked at me. "Mr. Carter's coming to visit tomorrow." He paused and laid the Bible

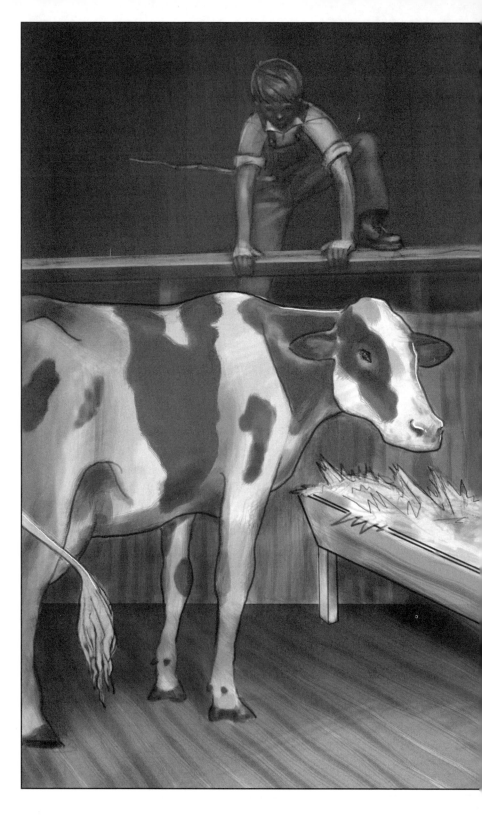

down. "He'll want to know if you like it here, and if we like having you."

I swallowed hard. "I do like it here."

He nodded. "You've been good help."

Mrs. Vogel looked up from her knitting. "And the good help best be getting on upstairs to bed now. Chore time comes early." Her needles had clicked all the way through the Bible reading.

I jumped up, remembering *The Adventures of Tom Sawyer* waiting for me upstairs. "Good night. And I'm sorry about scaring Bossy."

Mr. Vogel nodded. "She'll be okay. Just remember, farm animals are not toys. We depend on them."

Mrs. Vogel didn't pause in her knitting or look up. "Good night, boy."

As I climbed the stairs I realized neither Mr. nor Mrs. Vogel had said they liked *me* here.

CHAPTER 9

I leaned my head against Bossy's side and grasped the teat, squeezed, and pulled. The milk squirted into the bucket with a satisfying swoosh. I still couldn't work two at one time, but the bucket was filling.

I squirted more milk into the bucket. "Sorry I scared you yesterday, Bossy. I won't do it again."

She didn't look at me. Just kept chewing at the corn in her feedbox.

I pulled one more time, but there were only drops. Carefully I stood and carried the bucket out of the stall. Then I opened the stanchion to let Bossy loose, hung the stool on its peg, and gave her one last pat on the neck.

"I think you're my first real friend in Iowa." Her wet nose nuzzled my hands.

Mr. Vogel was outside of the barn working on the planter. He wiped his hands on a rag that hung from his back pocket. "Finished milking?" he asked.

"I got a whole bucket and didn't spill a drop." I held it out to show him.

"And it took you half the morning. I already fed the chickens. Take the milk to the missus and wash up for breakfast. You can gather the eggs after we eat."

I knew why we had to hurry. Mr. Carter would be here this morning. Would I have to pack up and leave with him?

For breakfast we had leftover biscuits topped with sausage gravy. Mrs. Vogel fried up some eggs too. We were quiet as we ate.

Mr. Vogel leaned back in his chair and sighed. "Good gravy, Pauline."

Mrs. Vogel had a first name too!

"Boy got a whole bucket of milk this morning. He did the milking himself." Mr. Vogel rocked a little on his chair.

Mrs. Vogel laid her fork down and looked at me. "Good. Glad to see you're pulling your share."

I squirmed in my chair, both warmed by the compliment and embarrassed by the attention. I stood and began putting things away. Mrs. Vogel joined me and we got the dishes washed and dried. When I started to hang up the dishtowel, she reached for it. "I'll take that. Why don't you put on the clothes you wore here, and I'll get those overalls and shirts washed."

I turned and trudged upstairs. Did she want me to put on the orphanage clothes so I'd be ready to go with Mr. Carter?

I was buttoning my shirt when I heard the sound of an automobile. I peeked out the window. It looked like Theodore was driving Mr. Carter again. I didn't bother with my shoes and ran downstairs.

Mrs. Vogel stood at the bottom, scowling. "We don't run in the house. Go back upstairs, put shoes on, and comb your hair."

With a sigh I turned and went back. When I arrived downstairs for the second time, Mr. Carter was in the kitchen shaking hands with Mr. Vogel, while Mrs. Vogel poured coffee into a fancy cup. I stood in the doorway and scuffed the toe of my shoe against the floor.

"There he is." Mr. Carter spoke in the jovial tone he used whenever prospective parents were around. "Come in, Bert, and tell me what you have been doing."

I stepped into the kitchen, and Mr. Carter reached out and ruffled the hair I'd just tried to comb down.

"I learned how to milk a cow."

Mr. Carter glanced at Mr. Vogel for a moment as if he didn't believe me, then he pulled out a chair. "Sit down, Bert." He looked at Mr. and Mrs. Vogel. "May I speak to him alone for a minute?"

"Sure." Mr. Vogel pulled back on the battered hat he wore outside. "We'll just be on the porch." Mrs. Vogel followed him out.

Was this when Mr. Carter would tell me he planned to take me back to New York? I eased into a chair. He sat across the table.

"You can be honest with me, Bert. Are the Vogels treating you well? Do you have plenty to eat?"

I was astonished. No one had ever asked my opinion of an adult. "Yes. I have my own room, and they gave me some clothes, and Mrs. Vogel makes the best fried chicken I've ever had."

Mr. Carter nodded and made some notes with a pen in a book he carried. "They don't beat you?"

I shook my head. "No. Not even when I do things wrong."

"That's good." Another note.

"Do you want to continue living here?"

"Oh, yes."

Mr. Carter made a final note in the book, stood, and reached across the table and shook my hand. "Glad to hear things are going well. Now you scoot along and stay out of the way while I talk to Mr. and Mrs. Vogel."

"Okay." I stood to go. "Mr. Carter?"

"Yes."

"How is Emma doing?"

Mr. Carter frowned. "Emma is fine. She is with good people who may decide to adopt her, so don't worry about her. Just stay out of trouble here."

Would my sister not be my sister anymore? I remember waking up and Mama was in her bed holding a blanket-wrapped bundle. She peeled back the corner of the blanket and told me then, "This is your sister, Emma. You must always look after her." I was the first person she smiled at. I was the one she tottered across the floor to as she learned to walk.

When Mama was sick, I'd get bread, and Emma and I would sit on the back stoop and eat slices for supper. And when we rode the train here, she slept with her head on my shoulder all night long. No matter what happened, Emma would always be my sister.

I stepped out onto the porch, closing the screen door quietly behind me. Mr. Vogel straightened from where he leaned against one of the pillars on the porch. "You can take the basket and get the eggs. Careful not to break any."

"Okay, Mr. Vogel." I picked up the basket from the porch and trotted toward the hen house. I could hear the screen door opening as the Vogels went inside for their meeting with Mr. Carter. What would they say? Would they tell him about all the things that I had done wrong?

I shooed the chickens away from the gate, just like I'd seen Mr. Vogel do. I fastened the gate securely behind me and then ducked into the little building with the slanting roof. Outside the chickens scratched and pecked and clucked. They didn't scare me anymore. I reached inside the first nest and found a still-warm brown egg. One for the basket. The next two nests were empty, but the third had one. This was kind of like a treasure hunt.

When the basket was nearly full, and I'd checked every nest, I headed back to the house. I set the basket on the porch floor and sat in the swing. The sound of Mr. Carter's voice drifted out. "Do you have questions?"

I could hear Mrs. Vogel's voice, but I couldn't understand the words. Should I move into the yard, so I couldn't hear? Instead I stopped the swing with my feet and tipped my ear to the window.

Mr. Carter's answer came clearly. "In that case, Bert will return to New York City."

My heart stopped as still as the swing. Then I slid off, and it creaked as it swung behind me. I ran from the porch to the barn. Inside I climbed the ladder to the hay loft and threw myself in the scratchy pile of loose hay. I cried, great shuddering sobs that shook my whole body. After a long time, I felt a soft furry body against my arm. I sat up and stroked the striped back. The kitten purred and rubbed its head against my leg.

"Where are you, boy?" Mr. Vogel's voice floated up to the loft. I brushed the wet tears off my cheek and started to wipe my nose on the sleeve of the shirt Mr. Carter had given me. But I'd have to wear the shirt on the train, so I used a wad of hay.

"I'm up here." I called.

"Well, what in tarnation are you doing in the hay loft?" His voice was cross.

"Just petting the kitten." I climbed down the ladder, leaping from the third rung.

Mr. Vogel frowned at my red eyes and mussed hair with hay poking out everywhere. "You need to change into your overalls. The missus wouldn't want you out here in those clothes."

"Where's Mr. Carter?"

"He told us to tell you goodbye and that he'll be back."

I kicked up a little cloud of barn dust and nodded without looking up. Mr. Carter would return to take me back to New York.

CHAPTER 10

All the rest of the day I wanted to ask when Mr. Carter would be back, but there just didn't seem to be a time. I helped Mrs. Vogel do the washing, carrying what felt like a hundred buckets of water for her to heat on the stove and pour into the tubs. One tub was for washing, one tub for rinsing. Then she hung the clean clothes on the clothesline in the side yard while I used the bucket to pour the dirty water outside.

After supper that night Mr. Vogel got out a wooden board and some homemade checkers. He laid them out on the kitchen table while Mrs. Vogel and I did the dishes and put away the food. I stuffed the towel over the rack.

"The towel won't dry like that. Straighten it out."

How had Mrs. Vogel seen where the towel was from clear across the kitchen? I took it off, folded it neatly in the middle, and rehung it.

"How about some checkers?" I thought at first Mr. Vogel was talking to his wife, but he was looking at me.

"I'm not very good. There was a board at Children's Aid, but the older boys got it most of the time."

Mr. Vogel rubbed his chin. "Then it's a good time to learn."

I scooted into the chair across from him. He beat me every game, but he told me where I should have gone, or how I could have played. Outside the sun slipped behind the barn and night crept across the barnyard.

"We better call it a night." Mr. Vogel said as he lit the kerosene lamp and handed it to me.

"Goodnight, Mrs. Vogel," I said as I passed through the front room.

She sat in her sewing chair with some material on her lap. She looked up and nodded. "Night, Bert."

Maybe Mr. Carter had told her my name. Or maybe she just remembered on her own.

As soon as I put my pajamas on, I blew out the lamp, climbed into bed, and fell asleep.

The next morning Mr. Vogel shook me awake. "Day's a-wasting, boy. We've got to get chores done before the missus walks you to school."

School. My eyes flew open. If I was to start school, Mr. Carter must not be coming for me today. I jammed my arms and legs into my clothes and raced downstairs for the bucket. I milked Bossy, let the chickens out in their yard, and fed the pigs.

For breakfast we ate oatmeal that Mrs. Vogel had sweetened with a spoonful of raspberry preserves. I ate two bowls.

"I'll take care of the dishes," Mrs. Vogel said. "You get your face washed and hair combed."

At the washstand I poured a little water from the pitcher into the basin and used the cloth to scrub my face, even washing my ears. Then I dried with the towel.

"Let me see." Mrs. Vogel tipped my chin and peered behind my ears. Then she lifted a hand. "Work on those hands some more. You look like you just came in from digging potatoes."

I used the soap and rubbed my hands until they were red. I dried them and held them out to Mrs. Vogel.

She nodded her okay, took off her apron, and put a perky blue hat on her head. She handed me a lunch pail. "Come on. You don't want to be late on your first day."

We walked down the lane. The sun shone over the green shoots coming through the ground. So different from New York streets and sidewalks.

A tiny yellow flower poked its head up and seemed to smile and nod at me. I bent to touch it. "Can I pick it?"

"Sure, it's just an old dandelion." Mrs. Vogel didn't stop.

I picked the bit of sunshine and tucked it in my overalls. Then I ran to catch up with her.

When we reached the white wooden schoolhouse, I stopped and stared. Kids ran around in every corner of the yard. Some swung high on a swing set and others spun on a merry-go-round. Beside the schoolhouse a couple boys threw a baseball back and forth, and more kids still walked up the road.

Suddenly I felt shy and wished I could grab hold of Mrs. Vogel like Emma used to grab me. I felt a hand on my shoulder and looked up at her. "Don't you be afraid, boy. You're as good as they are. You just came from a different place. You'll be okay. Put your chin up and march in there now."

So I did. I was almost to the steps leading into the schoolhouse when a whirlwind of skirts sped across the yard and wrapped around my waist.

"Bert, Bert. I'm so glad you came to my school." Emma buried her head in my chest.

I didn't care who was looking. I put my arms around her and gave her a hug back. We were still hugging when

a loud bell rang. I looked up, and the prettiest woman I'd ever seen was swinging the handle of a bell.

Emma slowly released me and pointed. "Girls line up here, boys over there."

I joined the line of jostling boys. Emma was wearing a blue dress that looked new, like something that would come out of a store in New York. She had shiny little black boots and blue ribbons in her hair.

I leaned over and whispered. "Do you like your family?"

Emma's smile was like the sunshine on the lane. "Yes. My mama sings songs and my papa takes me on his lap and reads me stories. I have a kitten that sleeps outside and a dolly and—"

"Emma Davidson." The pretty teacher frowned at my sister. "You know the rule. No talking when we line up."

"Yes, Miss Jones."

The line moved forward. Inside the boys and girls sat down at desks. The little kids, like Emma, were up front, the bigger kids in the back. I stuffed my hands in my pockets and rubbed the toe of one shoe against the other.

"And who might you be?" Miss Jones stopped beside me.

"Bert Davidson, ma'am. I'm staying with the Vogels just up the road. I would have been here yesterday, but I had to meet with Mr. Carter." Should I tell her he was taking me back to New York?

"Can you tell me what grade you're in?"

I hung my head. "I haven't been to school much. They taught me a little reading and ciphering at Children's Aid."

"I see. Why don't you sit in this desk next to Clarence? We'll have our opening exercises, then I'll work with you to see what group you'll best fit in." She moved to the front of the room.

Clarence glanced up with a quick smile. I sat at the empty desk and folded my hands on top.

"Class, this is Bert. Let's make him welcome to Harmony Hill School."

The entire room chorused, "Hello, Bert."

We stood and said the Pledge of Allegiance. Then we sang "My Country, 'Tis of Thee," and Miss Jones read a chapter from Proverbs about seeking wisdom.

"Your new spelling lists are on the chalkboard. Please copy them on your slates. Write each word three times."

Miss Jones pulled three books from a shelf by her desk and walked over. She opened the first one. "Bert, would you read this for me?"

It was a story about a crow and a fox. I read the whole page and only stumbled on the word *cheese.* Then she handed me the second book. It was harder, and she had to help me on three words.

The last book had a list of words at the top of the page. I didn't know what most of them were, and Miss Jones read them to me. Then I read the page about wasps. I remembered the words she'd told me when I came to them.

Miss Jones picked up the first two books and left the last one on my desk. "You will read with the third graders. It may be challenging at first, but if you work hard, I think you will succeed. Did you bring a slate with you today to do arithmetic?"

When I shook my head, she smiled. "If the Vogels don't have one, I have an extra you may use." She opened the reader to the page where I'd read. "Practice reading this entire selection to yourself so you'll be prepared when I call your group."

Then she went to the front where a row of chairs stood. She called the first graders for reading, and Emma glanced at me over her shoulder before she skipped up.

When it was time for arithmetic, Miss Jones handed me a slate. She wrote problems on the board. We were to copy them onto our slates and then solve them. I could do the first grade problems, but after that I was lost. And my fingers got tired of being counted on.

"Time for recess. Please line up in order at the door." Miss Jones finally announced.

I sighed with relief. I wasn't sure what the *order* was to line up, but I got into line behind Clarence and no one told me anything different.

Harmony Hill School was perched high on a ridge, and I was sure you could see most of the way to New York. The school yard had a few trees, but beyond them the fields spread out for miles. Far in the distance I could see the iron horse with the smoke from its breath floating behind. Was it on its way back to New York? Would I be riding it soon?

Emma raced up to me, holding hands with another girl about her age. "This is Charlotte. She's my best friend. And this is Bert. He's my big brother."

Charlotte, a round faced girl with blond braids, looked at me intently. "Why doesn't he live at your house?"

Emma frowned. "Cause he lives with someone else."

"I'm at the Vogels." I tried to explain.

"And I'm Emma Peterson." Emma swished her blue skirts.

When did she stop being Emma Davidson? But before I could ask, Charlotte tugged at Emma's hand. "Let's go swing."

"See you later, Bert." Emma and Charlotte raced off over the playground, leaving me alone under the tree.

CHAPTER 11

By the time we stopped for lunch, my head was spinning with numbers and words and letters. I'd gone to school a short time before Mama got sick, but then I stayed home to take care of Emma. We had some schooling at Children's Aid, but it wasn't an everyday all-day-long event.

After Miss Jones dismissed us, I pulled my lunch pail off the shelf and followed Clarence outside. We plopped down on an empty space on the steps.

Clarence looked at my pail. "What did your mom pack for you?"

"She's not my mom. I'm just living with them a while to help them out." I opened the lid to see what Mrs. Vogel had packed. There was a potato, still slightly warm from baking, a thick slice of bread spread with butter, some dried apples, and one of her oatmeal cookies. I felt like I was eating at the Mason Hotel.

After we ate, I joined the boys playing baseball. I'd played with a stick before, but I'd never seen a real bat. I didn't hit the ball the first time up to bat, but the second time I smacked it. The boys cheered for me just as if I were a real Yankee.

In the afternoon we learned about the Declaration of Independence. New York was one of the thirteen original colonies. Iowa was just Indian Territory then.

Miss Jones cleared her throat. "Boys and girls, I have a special announcement."

The class quieted. No one wiggled or scratched on their slate or raised their hand to go to the outhouse.

"The last day of school we're going to put on a program for our mothers and fathers. We'll have a spelling bee, and each of you will have a piece to recite."

Immediately an excited murmur rose from the desks, but not from me. Standing in front of people and reciting brought back a night I'd rather forget.

"Class, please raise your hand if you have a question."

Hands flew into the air.

"Can I wear my church dress?"

"Do we memorize our piece?"

"Will we have refreshments?"

Miss Jones answered every question but mine. I hadn't raised my hand, but I wanted to know. Would the program be held before or after I was returned to New York?

"Bert Davidson." For a moment I thought maybe Miss Jones had read my mind. "Please stay for a few minutes after the others leave. I'd like to visit with you. The rest of you may line up at the door."

There was a clatter of feet and lunch pails as everyone else lined up. Emma gave a little wave as she stood in line. Then the other kids walked out the door, and I sat at my desk in the empty classroom.

After a few minutes, while I listened to the shouts of the kids leaving, Miss Jones came back in. She sat in Clarence's chair and folded her hands on his desk. "I won't keep you long today. I know the Vogels will be looking for you. Tell me about yourself, Bert. Where did you go to school before?"

I talked. Miss Jones listened to me so well, I told her everything. How my mom had died, and I went to Children's Aid, and Emma and I rode the iron horse to Iowa.

"Emma is your little sister?"

"She used to be. But now she lives with the Petersons, and they're going to adopt her."

Miss Jones laid a cool hand on mine. "She'll always be your sister, Bert. Even if she has a different name; even if you don't see her."

I blinked fast. I didn't want to cry. "I won't see her when I go back to New York."

Miss Jones sat up straight. "Why would you go back to New York?"

"That's what Mr. Vogel and Mr. Carter said."

Miss Jones frowned, not like she was angry, but as if she were thinking really hard. "Well, until that happens, let's just act like you're going to be here forever. I can tell you're a smart boy. But there's a lot you've missed out on by not being in school. I'd like to help you catch up. I want you to talk to the Vogels about staying an extra half hour after school, so we can work on your math and reading skills."

"Thanks, Miss Jones. I'll ask, but I think they need me to help. That's why they took me in."

"I don't think that's the only reason they took you in. Do you believe in God?"

"God may be up there, but He doesn't care about me."

"Why would you say that?"

"He let my mom die, and now I'm losing my sister."

Miss Jones nodded slowly. "Yes, some really tough things have happened to you. But that doesn't mean God doesn't care. As a matter of fact, God cares for you more than anyone else ever could. I will be praying you come to see that. Now you better scoot home. The Vogels are probably looking for you. Goodbye, Bert."

"Goodbye, Miss Jones." I grabbed my lunch pail and hurried out the door.

I trotted down the road until I spotted the red barn. Then I sped up and ran all the way to the porch. I stopped to catch my breath.

The screen door opened, and Mrs. Vogel poked her head out. "How was school?"

"Great." I stepped into the kitchen and put my pail on the table. "Thanks for the lunch. It was good. Miss Jones wants me to stay after school. I told her I would ask you, but I might have to work." I looked out the window where the sun was low in the west. "Should I go milk?"

"I think you have time for a cookie." Mrs. Vogel handed me one and poured a glass of milk from the pitcher in the icebox. "Miss Jones wants you to stay after school? Did you misbehave?"

I swallowed the bite of cookie I'd been chewing. "She wants to help me with arithmetic. I'm not so good with my ciphering, and I can't read as well as some of the kids."

"Your schooling is what's important now. I'll talk to Roy about it. You finish up and then go on out and milk Bossy."

I gulped down the rest of my milk, grabbed the pail, and headed to the barn.

The familiar smell of hay and cow and grains hit my nose when I pushed open the door. Bossy mooed.

It felt like, well, it felt like home. I put food in the trough for Bossy, then let her in, stroking her soft neck as she moved past. I slid the stanchion closed and positioned myself at her udder. This time I tried two at a time. The milk almost poured into the pail, changing sounds as it filled from a sharp ping to a frothy shh.

As I was leaving the barn, the tiger kitty wandered in. I put the pail down a minute to stroke her. Then I carried the milk to the house.

Mrs. Vogel peered into the pail. "Looks like you did a good job. You got almost as much as Roy does."

"Where is Mr. Vogel?" I hadn't heard or seen him all the time I was in the barn.

"He started planting today. He won't be in until dark. You hurry out now and get the chickens shut in for the night, and here's the slop bucket for the pigs." She looked at me, then at the bucket of leftover food and milk. "Don't spill it."

Just when I'd finished all the chores, Mr. Vogel pulled into the barn yard. Edith and Forest were pulling a contraption behind them. It had a seat for Mr. Vogel and round sharp discs. Must be the plow.

He mopped his face with a bandana, then stuck it back in his pocket. "Hello, boy. Got the milking all done?"

"Yes, sir."

"Pigs fed? Chickens to bed?"

"Yes. Yes." I bobbed my head.

A grin flitted across his face. "Well, help me get these two hard workers put away, and we'll head in for some supper."

He drove Edith and Forest right into the barn. I helped hang the harness pieces in their place and put a scoop of oats in each of their feed bunks.

"Do they bite?" I asked.

"Never." He scratched behind Forest's ear and gave him a pat.

I touched the white spot on Edith's nose, but drew back when she raised her head and looked at me.

Mr. Vogel chuckled. "Go on, pet her. She's just an oversized kitten."

So I stroked the soft hair on her neck and watched her chew the oats.

"See?" Mr. Vogel said. "On this farm Edith and Forest are partners."

After one final pat I followed Mr. Vogel into the house.

Mrs. Vogel had made a stew with meat and potatoes, and we had biscuits again. After supper I helped with the dishes. When we finished, Mrs. Vogel picked up the dishpan. "Don't go upstairs yet, boy. Throw this water out, then I have something for you."

As I threw the soapy water around the bushes, then rinsed both dishpans the way she'd shown me, I wondered. Maybe another oatmeal cookie? Maybe a book from the shelf downstairs? I could hardly wait to find out.

I turned and ran back to the house. I'd dribbled some soapy water on the steps, and I slipped and scraped my leg. I squeezed my eyes shut to keep from crying out. Then I limped back in the kitchen and put the dishpans away.

Mrs. Vogel called from the front room. "Come in here."

When I walked in, she held up a blue plaid shirt just my size. I recognized the material that she'd been working on at night.

"Keen shirt." I wasn't sure whose it was or why she showed it to me.

"It's for you." Her face didn't, but her voice smiled.

"Thank you, Mrs. Vogel." I took the shirt and stroked the fabric. "I've never had anyone make a shirt just for me." Did this mean Mr. Carter would be here tomorrow? "Is it mine to keep?" I whispered.

"Certainly. You can wear it for school instead of those worn out shirts."

"Thanks, Mrs. Vogel."

Mr. Vogel peered over the top of the newspaper he was reading. "Night, boy. Looks like it will be another sunny day tomorrow. I'll be in the field at sunup. Can I count on you to do all the chores, the milking, the chickens, the pigs?"

"Yes, sir."

I carried my shirt upstairs and hung it carefully on the peg behind the door before undressing for bed. After I slid under the covers, I thought about Miss Jones saying God cared for me. But I still wasn't sure.

CHAPTER 12

Mr. Vogel called me when it was still dark. He used a match to light the kerosene lamp on my dresser.

After I put on my new shirt and stepped into my overalls, I trotted outside to use the outhouse. I could see Mr. Vogel by the barn harnessing Edith and Forest.

After I finished, I ran down. "Need my help?" I stroked Edith's velvety nose, and she lipped at my hand.

"I can take care of my team. You get the bucket. Bossy's waiting. I'll see you tonight." He tightened the strap around Forest's belly.

I trudged back to the kitchen for the bucket. After the chores were done, I washed up at the pump. Then I went inside and sat at the table.

Mrs. Vogel turned from the stove. "Would you bring me in another armload of wood? If you keep eating biscuits, I need more wood to bake them."

With my mouth watering I raced out and carried in a load so big, some of it spilled out on the kitchen floor. I dumped my armload in the bin, picked up the wood on the floor, and threw it in on top.

Mrs. Vogel took hold of my shoulders and held them for a moment, studying me. "The shirt fits you well." And this time her face smiled too.

"Yep. And I kept it clean while I did chores." I slid back into my seat at the table.

Mrs. Vogel brought two plates piled with ham, eggs, and biscuits. A third plate she kept on the stove for Mr. Vogel. She set our breakfast down and pulled out her chair. "Do you want to say grace?"

I'd taught Emma to pray, but I'd never prayed out loud that I could remember. No, I did not want to say grace, but I didn't think she was really asking if I wanted to. I thought of how Mr. Vogel prayed, as if God were sitting right at the table.

"Um. Thanks God for the biscuits and other food. Bless Emma and Mr. Vogel and Mrs. Vogel and me. Amen."

Mrs. Vogel was watching me when I opened my eyes. "Who's Emma?"

"She's my sister. She came on the train with me, but they gave her to another family. I got to see her yesterday at school." I poured a little molasses on my biscuit and licked my finger.

"That's nice you get to see her."

I wish we could live in the same house. I wish I could make sure she was being taken care of.

"She's all the family I got left."

Mrs. Vogel watched me bite into my biscuit, then she stood and checked something on the stove.

After I had scraped up the last bits of egg on my plate, I asked, "Do you need more wood before I go?"

"No. You go on to school and stay out of trouble."

I walked by myself this morning. I ran when I wanted, stopped to look at a bug, and picked up sparkly rocks.

When I turned in the schoolyard, I could see Miss Jones ringing the bell. Children raced from every direction to line up. I ran too, my bucket banging against my leg.

When I skidded to a halt, I almost bumped into a tall boy on the step ahead of me.

"Well, if it ain't the sissy boy from New York City." Frank Pearson sneered.

My heart sank. "You go to school at Harmony Hill?"

"When I ain't needed on the farm. Mr. Erickson has to get a part fixed for the tractor today."

Miss Jones frowned at us. "Remember, children, you're to be quiet."

The line of children moved inside and I waved at Emma as she flounced by in what looked like another new dress. This one was red, and she wore matching ribbons in her hair.

At recess Clarence and I joined a baseball game. While I waited for my turn at bat, Frank swaggered up. "Sissy boys don't play baseball."

I felt brave in my new shirt. "I'm no sissy boy."

Frank shrugged. "You look like a sissy boy to me. I hear you're at the Vogels' farm. They still use horses to plant corn."

"Yeah. So what? Edith and Forest are the best."

He tipped his head back and hooted. "At the Ericksons' we got us a Case tractor. We can plant the fields in half the time your old horse team takes."

I wanted to push his face in the dirt of home base.

Clarence, who was pitching, hollered at me. "You gonna bat or chitchat?"

I stepped up to the mark in the dirt that served as home plate. The first ball was slow and wide. I let it go past. Clarence spit in his palm, picked up a handful of the soft powdery dirt his feet had scuffed up, and rubbed it in. Then he reared back and threw the ball across the plate. I swung hard, but too late.

"Strike one." Clarence called.

He threw a second time, and I missed again.

"Strike two." Clarence grinned smugly.

I stepped back from the plate, scratched a bite on my leg, and stepped back up. Clarence nodded at the boy catching behind me. Then he leaned back and fired it off. I was ready. I swung the bat and connected. The ball soared up into the spring sky. I tossed the bat to one side and charged to first base, rounded it and started for second. I could see the ball out of the corner of my eye as it began its plummet to earth. The second baseman held out his glove and, smack, the ball dropped into it.

"Yer out." Clarence yelled. His team raced to line up to bat, as my team trudged out to positions on the field.

I could hear Frank laughing again. "Sissies can't play baseball."

I took my position at left field, my anger simmering. I could hardly keep my mind on the game. The other team scored two runs before the peals of Miss Jones's recess bell sounded.

"Tomorrow at noon. We're still up to bat." Clarence called as we raced to line up.

I was the first at the steps, but Frank was close behind me. I kept my eyes to the front. Emma and her friends had been jumping rope, and they lined up beside us, but she was giggling with the other girls and didn't wave or call to me.

Frank leaned forward and whispered in my ear. "She ain't yer sister anymore. She got herself a real mom and dad."

My hands knotted into fists at my side. I turned toward him and my arm came up, but at that moment, Miss

Jones brushed past me and handed Frank the bucket for our drinking water. "Please refill this from the well."

Then she walked into the classroom, and we followed. As I took my seat, my hands began to unfist, but the knot inside me remained. I didn't know how, but I would knock Frank Pearson flat.

Miss Jones wrote the arithmetic assignment on the board. I slid my slate out of my desk and began copying the problems onto it. I heard the thump when Frank set the bucket of water down and the rustle as he slid into his desk. I didn't turn around.

CHAPTER 13

I watched a robin carrying twigs to the tree outside the classroom window. The afternoon had dragged on like an all-day rain. I had daydreamed all through math about getting even with Frank. I had tried and discarded several options.

"Put your books away. That's all for today." Miss Jones brushed some stray hairs back from her face. "Frank Pearson and Bert Davidson, please stay. The rest of the class is dismissed."

The cold fear of punishment doused any burning embers of anger. Emma stood for a minute in the doorway before she turned and followed the others out. Miss Jones walked to the door and watched the rest of the children leave. Then she came and leaned against one of the desks that stood between Frank's and mine.

"Since you boys are new here, I'm going to be lenient with you. I don't know what grudges you brought with you." She stopped and looked at both of us. "You knew each other before today?"

We both nodded, and Frank for once kept his mouth shut.

Miss Jones cleared her throat. "I won't tolerate arguments being settled with fists. If you have a disagreement, and you've tried to work it out and haven't succeeded, that's when you bring it to me. I can act as a mediator. Do you understand?"

Our heads bobbed in unison, probably the first time we'd ever been in agreement.

Miss Jones stood and straightened her skirts. "Frank, for the remainder of the school year, you are in charge of our drinking water. I want the bucket filled every morning, I want you to check it at lunchtime, and I want it emptied before you leave in the afternoon."

"Yes, ma'am."

"That's all. You may go." Miss Jones turned to look at me as I listened to Frank's feet thumping down the aisle and out the door.

"Bert, I must say I'm disappointed in you."

Her words pierced me like tiny knives carving my heart. I wanted nothing more than to please my teacher.

"I didn't hit him."

"No, but you were going to."

She crossed the room and pulled a thick book off the shelf behind her desk. Then she walked over and laid it on my desk. "You are to read this entire book before the end of the term. I want a written, weekly report about what you've read and what you think about it."

I was confused. "That's my punishment?"

"Yes. Well, less of a punishment and more of a lesson." She touched the cover of the book. "I think you'll find some similarities in your situation and the events of this book. You may go now. We won't work anymore today."

I picked up the book and opened the cover so I could read the title. *Oliver Twist.* It was a big book. With a whole lot of pages. I'd start reading it tonight. I hoped I could get it read before Mr. Carter came to take me back to New York.

I tucked the book under one arm and started for home. I didn't run, because I didn't want to drop the book.

When I rounded the last hill and trudged down the lane, I could see Edith and Forest standing by the barn. The plow had been unhooked, but they were still in their harnesses. I slid the book inside my shirt, dropped my lunch bucket by the pump, and raced down to the barn. Edith greeted me with a soft whicker. I stroked her velvet nose and leaned my head against her neck for a moment. Horses weren't scary; they were the best kind of friends.

The barn doors creaked open, and Mr. Vogel strode out. He took hold of Forest's harness and led the team inside. Then he unbuckled the harness and lifted the parts to their pegs on the barn wall. He wiped the horses' backs with an old towel and checked them over for places where the harness might have rubbed.

"You can get them some grain in the feed troughs and a little hay too."

I raced to do what he asked. After both horses were in their stalls munching away on the grain, I walked with Mr. Vogel to the house. When the screen door banged behind us, Mrs. Vogel turned from the stove and wiped her hands on her apron.

"Well, here the two of you are all ready for coffee time."

Mr. Vogel gave me a gentle push. "Sit down there at the table. Pauline, pour me a cup of coffee and the boy some milk."

Mrs. Vogel filled a cup with coffee from the pot on the stove. Then she took the pitcher of milk from the icebox and poured a glass full. She set the coffee and milk on the table and went back to whatever she was cooking on the stove.

I took a big drink of milk, then looked at my fists in my lap. "How can I knock someone down who's bigger than me?"

Mr. Vogel set his coffee down so fast some of it sloshed out onto the tablecloth. "Why in tarnation would you want to knock someone down?"

Suddenly it all spilled out, my thoughts and words fluttering around like chickens in the yard. I told him how Frank always called me *sissy boy*, told me no one would take me in, and said Emma wasn't my sister anymore.

When I finished, neither of the Vogels said anything for a moment. Mr. Vogel sat turning his coffee cup around and around in his hands. Mrs. Vogel, who had come to the table when I started talking, wiped at the spot of coffee.

Then Mr. Vogel stood, planted both hands on the table, and leaned across toward me. "I don't care what this boy says to you. We don't want to hear of you fighting. That's not who you are. There's other ways of taking care of bullies. You hear?"

"Yes, sir." Not fight? How could I stand up for myself?

I reached into my shirt and pulled out *Oliver Twist*. "Miss Jones wants me to read this and report on it.

Mrs. Vogel reached for the book and thumbed through it. "That's quite an assignment."

I didn't mention that I thought she'd assigned it to keep me out of trouble.

"Finish your milk, boy." Mr. Vogel pushed the glass in front of me. "I hear Bossy. You can milk her and get the chickens shut in. I've got some repairs to do on the planter.

I drained the glass of creamy milk, grabbed the bucket, and hurried out to the barn.

CHAPTER 14

At school on Friday morning we began with the Bible reading, the Pledge of Allegiance, and a song. Then Miss Jones announced, "I have chosen your recitations for our program. We'll practice this afternoon, so let's all work hard on finishing our morning lessons."

An excited hum rose from the desks as we pulled out our slates. I thought about the night at the opera house, and a cold fear gripped me. How could I explain to Miss Jones that I couldn't get up in front of people and talk? Even if I was still in Oak Hill.

The morning slipped away faster than I wanted. At lunch Clarence and I sat under the tree, and I nibbled my biscuit and ham.

Clarence chattered happily, and I listened with only half my brain. The other half was trying to concoct ways to weasel out of doing a part in the program.

I laid the biscuit on my leg. "Have you been in one of Miss Jones's programs before?"

"Sure. We have one every year. She makes us practice until we're perfect. But the night of the program is fun. Lots of special food, and everyone comes, and we play games. You'll like it." He nodded emphatically.

I didn't think so. "What if someone can't do it?"

"You mean they're sick or something?"

"No. They just can't speak in front of people."

"Oh. Sometimes some of the younger kids get scared, but Miss Jones makes sure we know our parts so well no one forgets. I can still say mine from last year.

"Animal crackers and cocoa to drink,

That is the finest of suppers I think . . ."

He droned on. I watched Emma finish her lunch and join some girls skipping rope.

"Don't worry about Emma. She'll be fine." Clarence banged the lid of his lunch pail down. "Ready for baseball?"

I shook my head. "Not today. I'm trying to stay away from Frank." That was true. But not the real reason. My stomach was tied up in knots thinking about talking in front of people.

I hung my lunch pail on one of the hooks in the cloak room and reached in my bag for *Oliver Twist*. If I didn't play baseball, I might as well read. When Miss Jones rang the bell to signal the end of recess, I was deep into the story. Oliver was an orphan too. I knew exactly how he felt.

We took our seats quickly and waited while Miss Jones picked up some papers from her desk. She grinned like she had a stack of Christmas presents. "Boys and girls, these are your recitations. At the top of the page are your name and a number that tells you what order you will be in the program. Read your piece to yourself, then we'll read them out loud, and I'll answer your questions about the program. Be careful with the paper. This is your only copy."

She almost skipped around the room, handing out the papers. The other kids grabbed them like they'd been waiting all year for this. I took the paper she handed me and dropped it on my desk. My name and the number ten were written at the top. Underneath in bold capital letters was THE BEATITUDES. The same thing I'd tried to recite at the opera house! Could things get any worse?

All around me the other kids were reading their pieces in excited whispers. Looking at the long paragraph on my paper, I remembered. I hadn't been able to squeak out a single word, and I laid my head down on my arms.

Miss Jones said, "Boys and girls, let's begin." My head lifted slowly.

"Sarah will give the welcome." She motioned to her. "Go ahead, dear, stand up and read from your paper. We'll work on memorizing these later."

Sarah stood and flipped her braids over her shoulders. "Welcome to Harmony Hill School, parents, family, and friends."

I stared at the paper on my desk. I could stand and read it. That's what we did every day in reading class. I dug up every bit of courage I had as other classmates read.

"Bert, you're next. Number ten."

I stood and read slowly. I knew most of the words, just not what they meant. When I was finished, I plopped in my seat and listened as the rest of the children read. When everyone had finished, Miss Jones clapped her hands, and we joined in.

"A wonderful start, boys and girls. You may take your papers home and begin to memorize your piece. We'll practice every afternoon for the next month. Now don't forget your jackets. It's warm this afternoon, but it might be chilly tomorrow. You may line up at the door."

I stuffed the Beatitudes in my desk and pulled out my slate. The clatter of footsteps in the cloakroom and on the stairs faded.

Miss Jones walked to my desk and sat next to me. She'd been so kind to me. Maybe kinder than anyone else since Mama died. Maybe she'd understand why I couldn't do this.

I looked up and blurted, "Miss Jones, please, do I have to be in the program?"

She looked surprised. "Bert, why would you not want to be in our program? You did a nice job reading it this afternoon. And I'm certain you can memorize it."

"Yeah, I memorized it before. I just couldn't say it at the opera house."

She paused a moment before asking, "You memorized the Beatitudes to say at the opera house in Oak Hill? The night you came on the train?"

I nodded miserably.

"And you got a case of stage fright?"

I nodded a second time.

"I'm sorry I picked this piece for you. I had no way of knowing. I wasn't at the opera house that night. Would you rather I assigned you a different piece?"

I sighed. "I'd rather not be in the program."

She frowned and shook her head. "Oh, I don't think we can do that. The Vogels will come to see you, and they would be so disappointed if you didn't recite like all the other children. Let's look at it."

I took the paper from my desk and smoothed it flat.

Miss Jones pointed to the first sentence. "Do you know what the Beatitudes are?"

"They're from the Bible, aren't they?"

"Yes. They are a part of Jesus' Sermon on the Mount. They tell us how we should live to be truly happy."

I could be happy living on a farm in Iowa. I could be happy punching Frank Pearson in the nose.

I sighed. "I don't know how to be poor in spirit or meek or any of those things."

Miss Jones nodded. "It is a lot to take in, isn't it?" She was quiet for a moment, as if she were thinking. "Emma's verse sums it up rather well. Did you listen as she read today?"

"No. I was thinking about my piece."

"Tomorrow you listen to her read. Then see if you can practice doing what it says. In the meantime, try to re-memorize your piece. And if you truly feel you can't do it at the program, and you've told the Vogels ahead of time, I won't force you to recite."

This time I sighed with relief. "Thanks, Miss Jones."

Then she handed me my paper. "Go ahead and put this away. My hope is with enough practice you'll feel confident and choose to be in the program. I'm certain you can do this, Bert."

She might be certain, but I wasn't.

CHAPTER 15

Monday morning Mr. Vogel left early to plow the north field. When I started to school, I could see Edith and Forest leaning into their collars as they pulled the plow across the field. I waved, and Mr. Vogel waved back.

I stopped at the edge of the field and picked a handful of Sweet William for Miss Jones. She got all mushy over wildflowers.

I ran the rest of the way to school. Emma skipped over and gave me a huge hug, and I hugged her back. I didn't even care who was looking. Her eyes widened when she saw the Sweet William. "Are those for Miss Jones?"

"Yep, but I picked this one for you." I gave her the bright fuzzy dandelion I'd found in the school yard.

"Thanks, Bert." She took it and tucked it into one of her hair ribbons.

Miss Jones rang the bell, and we lined up at the steps. Frank watched us with a smirk, but he was too far ahead for me to hear any snide remark. My happiness evaporated as the heat of my anger toward him built inside.

As I took my seat, Frank put his hands on my desk and leaned over. "She's not your sister, so she must be a girlfriend," he taunted in a whisper.

My hands tightened into fists inside my overall pockets and I gritted my teeth, feeling like I was going to explode.

"Frank Pearson, take your seat." Miss Jones rapped her ruler on the edge of her desk, and he slunk off. My fingernails bit into my palms all during the morning prayer and pledge to the flag.

I spent the morning, when I wasn't reading or doing math, trying to figure out a way to get back at Frank. The anger boiled inside like the pots on Mrs. Vogel's stove. If she didn't lift them off the fire, the pots eventually boiled over.

The Sweet William. I'd left them in the cloakroom when I set my lunch pail down. I raised my hand and asked, "I left something in the cloakroom. May I have permission to get it, please?"

Miss Jones, busy with the squirmy first graders, answered, "Yes, you may, Bert."

I hurried out, then peeked back in the door. Miss Jones was busy teaching, and the other students were reading or practicing spelling. No one was watching me. I reached up on the shelf for the old rusty lunch pail I knew Frank carried to school. It held a potato and a small shriveled apple. I lifted the potato out and stuck it deep in the pocket of my jacket. Then I grabbed up the bouquet of wildflowers. I laid them on Miss Jones's desk and went back to reading my story.

Later Miss Jones came by my desk and thanked me for the flowers. For some reason it didn't make me feel great like I'd thought.

At lunch time I settled beside Clarence on the grass. I watched Frank as he opened his bucket. He pulled out that little apple and looked in the bucket again. Then he looked around him in the grass like he thought that potato could have hopped out of the bucket by itself. After a while he ate the apple slowly.

I ate my potato, biscuit, apple, and cookie, but they didn't taste as good as usual. When I scored a run in the baseball game at recess and everyone was slapping my back and calling me Babe, I still didn't feel happy. I felt small and mean.

Just as Miss Jones had promised, we finished social studies in time to practice. I took out my copy of the Beatitudes and studied them. When Emma's turn came, I remembered what Miss Jones said and paid attention.

Emma marched up, gave all of us a big smile, and read from her paper. "At Harmony Hill School we try to live by the Golden Rule. 'And as ye would that men should do to you, do ye also to them likewise.' Saint Luke 6:31." Then with a swish of her skirts that was almost a curtsy, Emma pranced off the stage.

Miss Jones smiled at her. "Good job, Emma."

As the next first grader took his place, I puzzled over the words Emma had recited. I glanced sideways at Frank standing at the end of the line.

I sure hadn't done that today.

On the way home I threw the potato into the field. It soared from left field to home plate, but I took no pride in it. When I stepped onto the porch, a wonderful warm smell drifted outside. In my hurry to get inside I almost let the door slam, but I caught it just in time.

Mrs. Vogel stood at the stove pulling out a cookie sheet. "I made snickerdoodles, Bert. Put your book bag and lunch pail away."

I'd never heard of snickerdoodles, but that didn't mean I wouldn't try one . . . or two or three, if they were offered. I hung my bag on the hooks and set the lunch pail on the counter. Then I sat down and waited while Mrs. Vogel scooped round cookies onto a rack.

She put three of them on a plate, poured a glass of milk, and set them on the table.

I bit into the crumbly, sweet, cinnamon treat. "You make the best cookies ever."

"Thank you, Bert. It's nice to have someone to bake cookies for." She spooned out dollops of dough onto the sheet. "How was your school day?"

"Okay. What does *poor in spirit* mean?"

She slid the cookie sheet in the oven, then pulled out a chair and sat at the table with me. "You mean like in the Beatitudes?"

"Uh-huh," I said around my cookie.

"Don't talk with your mouth full."

I swallowed. "Yes. Like in the Beatitudes."

"I think it means we're humble. We don't think too much of ourselves, and we put others first."

This time I made sure my mouth was empty first. "Kind of like the Golden Rule, right?"

"Exactly. Why do you ask?"

I shrugged and reached for a second cookie. "I'm memorizing the Beatitudes for our last-day program."

"Great. We'll look forward to hearing you recite." She stood up and went to the oven to peek at the cookies.

I decided not to tell her I wasn't going to be in the program. I swallowed the last of my milk, grabbed the pail, and headed for the barn.

CHAPTER 16

Only one week remained until our program at school. Mr. Carter hadn't returned for me yet, and some days I didn't even think about it.

I slipped *Oliver Twist* along with my last report into the bag Mrs. Vogel had sewed for me to carry my school books. I loved the story of Oliver, an orphan in London in the 1800s. I guessed I was glad I lived now, when people in Oak Hill, Iowa, would take you in, at least for a while.

I took the shortcut through the north field. After Mr. Vogel had plowed it with Edith and Forest, it looked like a giant slab of chocolate cake.

They'd be planting soon. He told me, "Edith and Forest are the best team around. You can't make straight rows unless you've got a good team."

When I entered the school yard, Emma came skipping up.

"Hi, Bert. I won't be here tomorrow."

I frowned. "Why not? Are you sick?"

"No. We're going to get up early and go to Des Moines. I have to stand before a judge, and he'll make me Emma *Peterson*."

I knew this was coming, but my stomach still twisted.

Emma took my hand like she used to when we still lived in New York. She swung my arm. "You'll still be my best brother, even if I am a Peterson."

I smiled down at her, but I felt like bawling. Would she even remember me when I went back to New York?

"Our program is just one week from Friday." Miss Jones announced after we'd said the pledge. "This afternoon we'll make invitations to take home to your parents. And we'll have rehearsals for the last thirty minutes of the day, starting today."

I took my reading book out and opened it to my story. The first graders, including Emma, marched up to the recitation bench. Emma held her book proudly. I could tell by listening that she was the best reader in the group. Good thing she lived in Iowa and wouldn't have to miss school and then try to catch up, like I did.

I pulled my thoughts back to my book and began reading. All the practicing Miss Jones had me doing made me a better and faster reader, but I still stumbled over some words.

Later in the afternoon, we all stood at the side of the classroom in the order of our recitations. The younger kids were first; the older ones were last, and I was tenth.

Sarah strutted to the front of the classroom where Miss Jones's desk usually stood and gave her welcome speech.

I'd practiced the Beatitudes until I could almost say them backwards. Miss Jones made me practice every evening before we worked on arithmetic, but I steadfastly refused to be in the program.

If I thought about it, the embarrassment of that night returned. Then I remembered the other feelings, the fear of no one choosing me and of wanting to belong somewhere. Even though I had a place to stay now, I didn't know for how long.

Sarah finished her speech and came to stand in the middle next to Clarence. One of Emma's friends, another first-grader, was supposed to go next. Emma gave her a little shove, and she shuffled to the front. She looked at Miss Jones, then over at us, then down at the floor.

Teddy bear has his lair
under Johnnie's rocking chair.
Pray take care, don't go there.
You will have an awful scare.

We snickered behind our hands.

When she ran back to the line, Miss Jones clapped and the rest of us joined in. "Next time, Dorothy, don't look at the floor. Look at your audience. Okay, who's next?"

One by one we said our pieces. Most of us had not only our own memorized, but everyone else's as well. The program would go off without a hitch.

After school I met with Miss Jones. We'd finished with subtraction, and now we were tackling multiplication.

"You've really improved in both your arithmetic skills and your reading." Miss Jones stood and walked to her desk. She returned with another book. "I thought you might like to take this home to read. You said you were reading *Tom Sawyer* at home. This one is by the same author. It's not a punishment, and you don't have to write any reports." She smiled as she handed me the book.

Huckleberry Finn. I looked at the author's name. Mark Twain. Maybe someday I would write stories and put them in a book for boys to read.

I put the book inside my bag along with my jacket and picked up my lunch bucket. "Bye, Miss Jones," I called as I started out.

When I got to the trees along the fence row, a movement in the brush caught my eye. I stooped under the trailing branches of the tree to investigate. Curled up under a sticker bush was a dog. I wasn't particularly fond of dogs. Those that roamed the streets of New York City were mostly thin, mean strays intent on finding food to stay alive. I'd had my hand bitten when I reached into a garbage can that a burly black dog considered his.

This dog turned its head from me and cowered down. I could tell it was afraid of me, and I wondered why it didn't run away. I crept closer. Dirty, blond fur covered its body. A ragged rope was wound around its neck and tangled in the thorns. The dog not only couldn't run away, it couldn't move.

"It's okay doggy, I won't hurt you." I spoke softly, and the dog's long tail thumped against the ground. I stretched out my hand slowly. After regarding me for a few moments with dark eyes, the dog stretched out and gave my hand a quick sniff, then its tongue snaked out and licked me.

"I'll get you untangled." I pulled on the rope and pushed at the branches, gasping as the sharp thorns raked across my hands. The brambles held the rope tight. If I had a knife, I could have cut the rope, but I didn't. As my fingers worked at the knot, the dog whimpered softly and tried to rise to its feet.

I stopped for a minute and stroked the soft flaps of its ears. "I'm trying to help, really I am." I tugged at the rope again and felt the knot loosen slightly. I slid my finger under and pulled. At last it gave way, and the end of the rope dropped to the ground.

For a moment, not realizing it was free, the dog lay still. Then using its paws to pull and scoot on its belly, it crawled out of the bush and into my lap. I stroked its head and back. I checked, and she was a girl. Her legs were covered with small cuts and injuries. The thick fur around her neck almost hid a long red welt where the rope had rubbed her neck raw.

She lifted her head and began licking my face. I fell backwards and giggled. More licks, and now her tail whipped like Mrs. Vogel's washing on the clothesline. I pushed to my feet and picked up my bag that I'd dropped in the grass. "I have to get home, girl. You'd better go home too."

She just stood, looking up at me. I started across the field. I hadn't gone far, when she trotted after me.

I wondered what Mr. Vogel would say when I walked into the yard with a dog following me. Maybe he'd know where she belonged.

Or maybe he'd let me keep her.

CHAPTER 17

Mr. Vogel took off his hat and ran his fingers through his hair. "She could be part border collie, but those short legs look like a cattle dog."

I tried to act like it didn't matter to me. "Do you think she belongs to someone around here?"

"Enos Taylor has some herding dogs. She might be his. He doesn't have a reputation for taking care of his animals."

I parted the fur on her neck to show him the wound the rope had made. "Should we put something on this?"

"In the barn there's some udder cream I use on Bossy. That'll take care of it."

I turned toward the barn.

"Boy."

I stopped and looked back at Mr. Vogel.

"We'll have to tell Enos his dog is here. Don't go getting attached to her, cause she's not going to stay."

"Yes, sir, I won't."

I found the udder cream on the shelf in the barn and rubbed it gently onto the sore places on the dog's neck, and she washed my face with her tongue. I plunked down in the straw on the floor, and she turned around once and lay down, her head in my lap. I stroked her head. I'd lied to Mr. Vogel. I was already crazy about this dog.

She followed me around all the time I did chores, waiting outside the chicken pen and then beside Bossy's stall. When I carried the milk into the kitchen, Mrs. Vogel handed me a plate with meat scraps and some leftover biscuits. "Give this to the dog. She looks like she's been starved."

"Come on, girl. Here's some food." I set the plate down on the porch. It was gone in a few seconds. The dog licked at the empty plate and scooted it around the porch floor.

When I carried the plate back in and handed it to Mrs. Vogel, she pointed to an old rug on the floor. "You can put this on the porch for her to sleep on."

I laid the rug down and patted it. "You can sleep here." The dog wagged her plume of a tail, turned around once on the rug, and flopped down with a sigh. I gave her one more hug and hurried inside where I thought I smelled leftover ham slices sizzling in the skillet.

Mr. Vogel said the prayer, then carefully buttered a biscuit. "I'll be making a trip over to Enos Taylor's in the morning. You can ride along, if you like."

I nodded and swallowed the mouthful of ham I'd been chewing. "What if it's not his dog?"

"Dog belongs to somebody, or she wouldn't have a rope around her neck."

"But he hurt her."

Mr. Vogel sighed. "Doesn't make any difference. If she belongs to someone else, we don't keep her."

Mrs. Vogel passed the dish of green beans. "We don't need another mouth around here to feed anyway. I can barely keep food on the table for the two of you."

But after we finished washing and drying the dishes, Mrs. Vogel handed me another plate full of scraps. "She looks like she could use more food."

The dog wolfed the contents of this plate down even more quickly than the first one. I sat on the porch and petted her for a while. Then when it began to get dark and chilly, I patted the rug. "You lie down on this, girl, and I'll see you in the morning."

Her eyes followed me as I went inside.

Mr. Vogel had lit the kerosene lamp in the front room. The Bible lay open beside him. Mrs. Vogel worked on the fabric in her lap. She looked up at me over the glasses perched on her nose. "You took your time. We've been waiting on you for our reading."

I slid into the chair. "I waited while she ate. She likes your food."

Mrs. Vogel made a noise in her throat. "Humph."

I wasn't sure if she was angry or just letting me know they'd been waiting.

Mr. Vogel picked up the Bible. "I'm reading tonight from Saint Matthew, the fifth chapter. The Sermon on the Mount."

The first part was the Beatitudes. I could say them, even in my sleep. Why didn't I remember them that night at the Mason Hotel?

Mr. Vogel had a great voice, deep and not too loud. I loved listening to him read in the evening.

After the Beatitudes, he read about how we were salt, and then I wasn't listening for a while. There was a moth at the window, trying to get in to the lamp. He fluttered across, then fluttered back. I thought I could almost hear his little wings against the glass.

". . . 'but I say unto you, Love your enemies, bless them that curse you, do good to them that hate you, and pray for them which despitefully use you, and persecute you.' "

"What?"

Mr. Vogel stopped reading and stared at me. Mrs. Vogel dropped her sewing on the floor.

"Could you read that part again? The part about people that hate us?"

Mr. Vogel cleared his throat. Then he reread the verse. "Want me to go on now?" he asked.

I nodded, and he finished the chapter, closed the Bible, and laid it on the end table. "That's a hard thing to do, to love our enemies."

"My sister, Emma, says the Golden Rule in the program. It says we're to treat others like we want them to treat us."

"Yes. Jesus tells us to do some hard things, but they're for our benefit."

"About time for you to head upstairs." Mrs. Vogel had her eyes on her sewing again, but I knew who she was speaking to.

"Can I say good night to the dog?"

"If you're quick about it."

I hurried out to the porch. The dog was sleeping on the rug. She raised her head, and her tail thumped on the floor boards.

I stroked her golden head. "We're supposed to love our enemies and do good to them. I guess that means you have to love whoever hurt you, girl. And I have to do good to old Frank Pearson. Ugh." Her tail thumped again. "Time for me to go to bed now. Night, girl."

As I started upstairs, I felt something rustle in my pocket. I turned around and went back down. "I forgot to give you this. We made them today."

We'd used construction paper and crayons to decorate our invitations. Then we'd carefully printed:

Please Come To Our
Spring Program

May 15th, 1929

5:00 p.m.

Potluck following

I'd signed my name *Bert Davidson.* I handed it to Mr. Vogel. He read it, then gave it to Mrs. Vogel to read.

"We'd be honored to come to your spring program, Bert." Mr. Vogel said.

Mrs. Vogel had a sad look on her face, and she seemed to see something far away. I turned and started back upstairs.

Still holding the invitation, Mrs. Vogel called after me. "Yes, we'll both be there."

I just hoped Mr. Carter wouldn't come for me before the fifteenth.

CHAPTER 18

My feet thumped onto the chilly wood floor. I quickly pulled on my overalls and shirt and smoothed the quilt over my pillow.

Saturdays were working days on the farm, and I loved them. Sometimes Mr. Vogel and I worked on the machinery, the plow, the planter, or some of the smaller tools. Sometimes we fixed the fences. There was always wood to cut or split. I was now in charge of using the small hatchet to cut kindling for the stove, and I kept the wood box full.

In the kitchen Mrs. Vogel stirred something that smelled like oatmeal. I hoped she'd sprinkle mine with raisins like she had the last time.

Then I remembered the dog. Had she slept all night on the porch? Was Mr. Vogel really going to take her home this morning? I stepped toward the door to peek out.

Mrs. Vogel spoke without turning around or pausing her stirring. "Dog's following Mr. Vogel with his chores. Go get to the milking. The oatmeal's almost done."

"Yes, ma'am." I grabbed the bucket and hurried outside. I cringed when the door made a little slam, but Mrs. Vogel seemed too busy with the oatmeal to notice.

The dog stood down by the barn. When she saw me, her head went up, and she just stared for a moment. Then with her yellow tail going like crazy she ran to me, leaping around me like a giant furry grasshopper. I gave her a hug, scratched her ears, and checked out the wound on her neck. It looked better. I'd put some more udder cream on it after milking.

The dog followed me into the barn and stood with her nose poked between the boards of Bossy's stall as I milked. Then she followed me back to the house.

I set the bucket of milk on the counter, and Mrs. Vogel handed me an old pan with some scraps. She poured a bit of the milk on it. "Hate to give an old dog good food," she grumbled.

"She's not an *old* dog," I protested as I maneuvered carefully out the door, careful not to let it bang or to spill the contents of the pan.

I set the scraps down on the porch, and the dog dove right in.

Mr. Vogel was at the well. He pumped a stream of water and washed off his hands, rubbing them in the cold water. Then he splashed some on his face. "That oatmeal ready?" he asked me.

"I think so."

Then as we walked toward the house, he put an arm around my shoulders. It was the best morning ever.

There were raisins in my oatmeal. As we ate, Mr. and Mrs. Vogel chatted about the garden and the neighbors, and I tuned out. I thought I heard the dog flop down on her rug on the porch. After breakfast I was going with Mr. Vogel to take her back. Would her owner keep tending the wound? Would he tie her up again? Would he feed her better?

Mr. Vogel stood, and his chair scraped back. "You about ready to go, boy?"

I tipped the last of the cream in the bowl into my spoon and ate it. I wished I could use my tongue to lick the bowl the way the dog did. "Sure. But don't I need to help with the dishes first?"

Mrs. Vogel made a shooing motion with her hand. "Go on. There aren't that many, and I can do them."

Mr. Vogel hitched up Edith and Forest to the wagon. I whistled for the dog, and she came running from the side of the barn where she'd had her nose buried in the long grass. I climbed onto the seat, and she leapt up and sat between my legs. She looked delighted to be going on a trip. I wasn't feeling quite as joyful, more like I was betraying a friend.

Mr. Vogel handed me a rope. "Put this around her neck, just in case she decides she wants to jump out before we get there."

I looped the rope around, carefully avoiding the wounded area. She licked my hand, and I stroked her. Maybe if I showed him the sore, maybe if I pointed out where her ribs showed, maybe he would take better care of her.

Mr. Vogel guided the horses in the opposite direction from the schoolhouse. I hadn't been on this road since the train brought me to Oak Hill weeks ago. Now green grass waved beside the road, pink wild roses bloomed in the ditch, and in the fields the corn made stripes in the black dirt. Mr. Vogel pointed out a meadowlark perched on a fence post. The bird with the bright yellow belly puffed out his chest and whistled his four note song. He didn't have stage fright at all.

We turned onto a narrow, rutted lane. Even though Mr. Vogel slowed Edith and Forest, the wagon tipped from side to side, and I bounced on the wooden seat. I clutched the narrow metal hand rest with one hand and the seat with the other.

At last Mr. Vogel said, "Whoa," and the horses stopped. I felt like I'd been in Mrs. Vogel's gas-powered washing machine. After my body parts all settled back together, I looked around. The wagon was parked in front of a small, faded gray house. A few chickens scratched about in the dirt. Up ahead an unpainted barn, not nearly as large as ours, stood circled by a hodgepodge of small outbuildings. The sound of barking came from the direction of the barn.

I looked down at the dog. She'd crawled under the seat, and now she peered up at me.

"She doesn't act like this is her home." My stomach felt like it might get sick.

Mr. Vogel wrapped the end of the reins around the brake handle and stepped down from the wagon.

The screen door banged, and a short man in a dirty straw hat stepped out on the porch. He raised one arm in greeting.

Mr. Vogel crossed the yard. "Howdy, Enos. Are you by chance missing a dog? We had one show up at our place. We thought she might belong to you."

The man rubbed a bristly chin. "Blonde dog? Short legs? Yeah. She ran off a couple days ago."

Mr. Vogel looked up at me still in the wagon. "Bring the dog on down here."

I climbed out of the wagon. The dog crept further under the seat. "Come on, girl," I called. She turned her head. I took the rope and tugged a little. Head down and tail tucked between her legs, she slunk out. I tugged again, and she leapt from the wagon.

I walked over to where the men stood.

Mr. Vogel put his hand on my shoulder. "This is Bert Davidson. He's been taking care of your dog. Bert, this is Mr. Taylor."

I handed the rope to Mr. Taylor. "Here's your dog, sir."

He took the rope, and the dog twisted her head and licked his hand. He didn't pat her or anything, but she wagged her tail a little as she looked up at him. Was she *turning the other cheek and loving her enemies?*

"I found her tangled in the bushes of our tree line in the north field, and then she followed me home. Look, her neck's sore." I parted the fur to show him the wound.

"Yeah. Gotta tie this dog up to keep her at home. She likes to roam."

Mr. Vogel gave the dog a brief pat on her head. "We're glad to find where she belongs." Then he gave me a little nudge toward the wagon. "We better be going now. I have to go to town."

I took a couple steps toward the wagon, then stopped. "You'll take good care of her, won't you Mr. Taylor? She's a good dog."

He looked at me without smiling. "I don't coddle my dogs."

I stumbled the rest of the way to the wagon. Mr. Vogel unwound the reins and clicked his tongue at Edith and Forest. I turned and watched the dog until the wagon was too far away.

When we were back on the road, Mr. Vogel handed me the reins. "Want to try driving?"

I took them, feeling the power of the two big horses. Mr. Vogel showed me how to pull the reins to make the horses stop or turn. He talked to them too, as if they understood every word he said.

Soon we could see houses and buildings. Mr. Vogel took over the reins, and the horses slowed as they approached the main street of Oak Hill. The road turned to brick, and their hooves made a clomp, clomp sound. Another wagon passed us going the opposite direction. Edith neighed hello.

We pulled up to Glen's General Store and Grocery, and Mr. Vogel reached into his pocket, pulled out a list, and handed it to me. "Take this in and tell Glen it's from Mrs. Vogel. He'll fill it while we're at the blacksmith's, then we'll be back to pick it up and pay for it."

I scrambled down and ran into the store. A small bell tinkled over the door, and a small, thin man appeared from the back, wiping his hands on his apron. "What can I do for you, son?"

I handed him the list. "This is from Mrs. Vogel. Mr. Vogel and I are going to the blacksmith's, and we'll be back."

The man gave me a little salute like soldiers do. "Yes, sir."

I laughed as I hurried back to the wagon. We drove two blocks to the blacksmith's. There was another wagon and a horse tied up outside, and Mr. Vogel tied up our horses alongside them. Inside, a big man with broad shoulders stood at an anvil hammering on a large horseshoe, still red-hot from the fire. He tapped it here and there, changing its shape gradually until he was satisfied and dunked it in a tank of water. The horseshoe sizzled and hissed, and little clouds of steam rose from it.

He turned, wiped his hands on the sides of his pants. "Hello, Roy. Who's this you got with you?"

Mr. Vogel put his hand on my shoulder again, and I stood up tall. "This is Bert. He's my helper on the farm now."

The blacksmith held out a giant hand, still black from the hammer. "Nice to meet you, Bert." He pumped my hand up and down. "My name's Ted."

"Nice to meet you, Mr. Ted. I've never met a real blacksmith."

He threw back his head and laughed. "Well, what can I do for you today?"

Mr. Vogel handed him a part to the planter. "This canister has almost rusted clear through. Can you make a replacement? I don't need it this year. Corn's all in."

Mr. Ted took the part and turned it over in his hands. "Let me check, Roy. I may have a spare one here." Then he went to a stack of metal parts and pieces in the back corner. After a few moments, he returned and handed Mr. Vogel the part.

"Well, that saves me a trip here. What do I owe you, Ted?"

Mr. Vogel paid the blacksmith while I gazed around the shop. There were glowing embers of the fire, giant-sized billows, an anvil and hammer, and piles of metal everywhere.

"Would you like to help me do the other shoe?" Mr. Ted asked me.

I looked at Mr. Vogel. He nodded. "We're not in a hurry today."

I stepped up by Mr. Ted. He lifted the shoe with a long pair of tongs. "You run the bellows. Just pull that cord when I say *go* and stop when I say *stop*."

When he said *go*, I grabbed the cord hanging from the bellows and pulled. Again and again. The fire in the kiln blazed up. Mr. Ted shoved the shoe right into the middle of the pile of coals. Just when my shoulder was beginning to ache, he said *stop*. Then he pulled out the shoe with the tongs. It glowed bright red. He laid it on the anvil and handed me the hammer. I grunted with the effort of lifting it. He pointed at the shoe. "Hit it right there."

The hammer hit the hot shoe, sparks flew, and it bent a little. Mr. Ted nodded, then reached for the hammer. He hit the shoe a hard whack, then followed with little taps here and there until he was satisfied. Then he dunked it in the tank of water and left it sizzling as he shook my hand.

"If you ever get tired of farming, I'll take you on as my apprentice." He chuckled.

"Thanks, Mr. Ted." I followed Mr. Vogel out of the shop.

We picked up two boxes overflowing with groceries from the store. I helped carry them out, then Mr. Vogel handed me a penny. "Go get yourself a bag of candy."

I looked at the penny, then at Mr. Vogel. I'd never had a whole penny's worth of candy all to myself before. Maybe I could share with the Vogels or take a piece in my lunch bucket for Emma.

I chose butterscotch drops, and as I settled back on the wagon seat, I popped one in my mouth and let it melt slowly on my tongue. I offered the bag to Mr. Vogel, but he said, "No, thanks."

We were out of town before I remembered the dog. I missed her.

CHAPTER 19

Turn the other cheek. Do good to them that hate you. Love your enemies. The words flopped around in my head like the chickens in the yard as I walked to school Monday morning. Could I really do good to Frank Pearson?

Miss Jones stood on the steps ringing the bell, and I ran the rest of the way to the schoolyard. As we filed inside, Frank whispered over his shoulder, "Almost late to school. Weren't you finished in the kitchen, sissy boy?"

I bit back the retort I wanted to say. "I was helping Mr. Vogel hitch up the horses. Maybe we need a tractor."

"Course you do," he snorted. Then both of us quieted as we entered the classroom.

At lunch time I nibbled on my baked potato. Mrs. Vogel said the new potatoes would be ready soon. I hoped so. This one was kind of shriveled and had some brown spots. I glanced at Emma. She had a white bread sandwich with some kind of meat filling.

I'd put two of my butterscotch drops in the bottom of my lunch pail, thinking maybe Emma and I could sit and eat our candy together. I didn't really want to be seen sitting with the girls, but I missed my sister. I wanted to hear about her trip to Des Moines and getting adopted.

I swallowed the rest of my potato, went over, squatted beside her, and held out a butterscotch drop. "I got these Saturday at the General Store in Oak Hill. I saved this for you."

"Thanks, Bert." She took the candy. "We go to town every Saturday. Mama usually gets me a licorice stick."

My heart twisted when she said *Mama*. I knew she didn't remember her real mother, but I did. I took the other butterscotch drop and started to unwrap it. And then I saw Frank. He was sitting all by himself. He never had much lunch, just a biscuit or potato.

Do good to them that hate you. I sighed and rewrapped the candy. I walked over and handed it to Frank.

"What's this for?" He sounded like I'd just handed him a lizard.

I shrugged. "Just thought you might like it." Then I walked out to join the guys forming the baseball teams for recess.

When Frank joined the group, he was on the other team. But when he hit the ball for a double, I told him, "Good hit. You really smacked it."

At the end of the day, we had a run-through of the program. Miss Jones said we'd practice every afternoon this week.

As we lined up, Frank elbowed me. "I hope you don't mess up and forget your lines like you did at the Mason Hotel."

I just grinned and replied, "I hope I don't either."

Then after school I raised my hand and waved at him. "Bye, Frank. See you tomorrow."

I jogged most of the way home on the road. It had rained on Sunday, and I didn't want to wade through the mud in the field. I hoped there would be a cookie to go with the glass of milk Mrs. Vogel always handed me when I got home. My favorite was the crispy gingersnaps.

When I trotted up on the porch, I got a little bit sad when I saw the rug the dog had used. I wondered if the sore on her neck was healing and if anyone was petting her.

I eased the screen door shut behind me and put my lunch pail on the counter. There was a glass of milk on the table, but no cookie. I sat down and drank a little. The cool, creamy beverage tasted great after running most of the way home.

Mrs. Vogel came in from outside, wiping her hands on her apron. "There you are. I have an errand for you to run."

I wiped my mouth on one sleeve. "Sure? What?"

"Mr. Vogel took the team to the north field today to pull some stumps. He came back for lunch, ate just a bit, but hasn't come in for coffee time. I thought he might want a little something to eat this afternoon." She held out a sack. "And there's a cookie in there for you too."

I took the sack and started off around the barn and into the corn field, walking in the grass at the edge to avoid the mud. I found a stick and picked it up, thinking I could use it to fend off an enemy. A robin carrying a twig in her mouth fluttered in one of the trees along the fence line. I stopped and watched as she wove it into the beginning of her nest. Further on I heard a buzzing and found a bee's nest in the ground with little fat bees flying in and out. I considered poking my stick in the hole but thought better about it. My stomach grumbled. I remembered the cookie and walked on.

As I topped the hill, I could see Edith and Forest, their round, black shapes like mounds of dirt at the edge of the field. They didn't move, except as I got closer I could see their tails swish over their backs, shooing away the flies. I couldn't see Mr. Vogel anywhere. Was he taking a break?

I moved a little faster, not stopping to see where the green garter snake that slithered across my path went or to pick up the red rock. I broke into a trot, then a run as I approached the team, slowing only when they threw up their heads to watch me. Edith whinnied, and Forest shifted his weight from one foot to the other.

"Whoa, Edith, it's just me. Whoa, Forest, old boy."

"Bert." Mr. Vogel's voice croaked from somewhere behind the horses. I stepped around Forest. The horses' harness, instead of being hooked to a wagon, had heavy chains fastened to it. These chains were wrapped around a stump that was as big around as I was tall. The stump, partially pulled from the ground, sat on its edge with the roots like monster claws behind.

"Over here, boy." I went to the other side and then I saw him. Mr. Vogel's bottom half was under the stump, so only his head, chest, and arms showed. His face was an odd gray color.

My eyes filled with tears as I rushed to him. "What can I do?" I grabbed his arm. Could I pull him out?

"No." He groaned. "I'm pinned under the stump."

Somehow he'd gotten into the hole as the remains of the tree came out. The weight of the stump was against his leg. If the horses moved forward, they would crush it. I threw myself against the stump and pushed. It didn't budge. Forest stomped one foot.

I squatted down by Mr. Vogel. "If I unhook the horses and take them around to the opposite side, I think we could pull the stump back the other direction. Then I can get you out."

He nodded, his jaw tight. "Hold onto Forest. He's nervous."

I went to work unhooking the chains from around the stump. My hands fumbled with the thick metal loops. "God, help me do this. And help Mr. Vogel be okay." The prayer came without thinking from somewhere deep inside.

The last hook was undone, and the loose chain dropped to the ground. Forest quivered and took a step forward.

"Whoa, boy." I grabbed the reins just as Forest moved out. My only experience driving the team had been in the wagon with Mr. Vogel sitting beside me. Now he lay in a hole with a stump on his leg, and it was up to me to free him.

I stepped behind the horses and clicked my tongue. "Get on up there, Forest. Giddyup, Edith."

The horses began walking, the chains dragging and clunking along behind. We walked out into the field a ways before I pulled the rein to turn, hoping they wouldn't continue to the barn.

They circled back toward the stump, following my directions just as if I were Mr. Vogel. I had to stop, start, and turn a few times before I had them lined up facing the opposite direction. "Whoa." I hollered, and they stopped. Mr. Vogel was silent. Was he still alive?

Rushing to refasten the chains around the stump, I tripped and sprawled face first in the dirt. I scrambled to my feet, grabbed the chain, and lugged it around.

As I maneuvered it past Mr. Vogel, his eyes fluttered open. "Hurry," he whispered.

I hooked the chains together and picked up the reins. The horses needed to pull enough to relieve the pressure on his leg, but not far enough to topple the stump back in the hole.

"Giddyup, Forest, Edith." They strained forward, the chain tightening behind them. "Come on you two, pull!"

The stump trembled and moved.

Mr. Vogel's scream tore through the air.

"Whoa. Hold it there." I raced back to his side.

He waved his hand at me. "Go on, just a bit farther."

I picked up the reins again. "Come on, Forest. Come on, Edith." Their muscles rippled under their skin as, heads lowered, they pushed into their collars. The stump rustled and cracked behind me. I stopped the horses again.

Mr. Vogel was using his hands to lift and drag his body. I put my hands under his shoulders and pulled. His face went white, but working together we got him out of the hole and away from the stump.

He opened his eyes. "John, take the team back and get the wagon. Mom will help you. Go on now, I'll be okay. Hurry."

John? Why did he call me John? It didn't matter. I unhooked the chains without fumbling this time. They dropped to the ground, and I shouted, "Giddyup, Forest. Giddyup, Edith." I ran behind them around the outside of the field and into the barnyard.

CHAPTER 20

"Mrs. Vogel! Mrs. Vogel, he's hurt bad." I shouted, even though I was panting so hard I could barely get the words out.

Mrs. Vogel came running from the house. She even let the screen door bang behind her.

"In the field. Wagon. Get him in the wagon." Tears ran down my face, and I wiped at them with my dirty hand.

Mrs. Vogel took hold of my shoulders. "Can you hitch the team up?"

I bobbed my head, sniffing. "I think so."

"I'll get supplies." She ran to the house.

I unwound the chains, and they dropped to the ground. Edith and Forest turned their heads to the barn. "Not yet, guys. You have more work to do."

I used the reins and guided them to the wagon. "Back, back, back." They stepped into position, and I hooked them to the doubletree. I had them almost all hitched up by the time Mrs. Vogel arrived with blankets and a bottle of water tucked under her arm.

"There's a pile of boards in the barn. Do you know where they are?"

I nodded. "By the grain room."

"Bring two of them, long enough to make a ramp from the back of the wagon to the ground."

I took off as she checked to make sure I'd hitched up correctly. I slid the boards in back and climbed up to the seat beside her. She handed me the reins.

Forest and Edith started off without a shake of the reins or a *giddyup* or anything. They must have known it was an emergency.

When we got to the field, I pulled the horses to a stop. Fear froze my insides. Mr. Vogel lay so still. His eyes were closed and his face pale. Mrs. Vogel jumped from the wagon and hurried over to him. I wrapped the reins around the brake and followed her.

His eyes fluttered open, and when he saw Mrs. Vogel, he smiled a tiny bit. "I slipped. Bert pulled me out." He moved as if he were going to sit up, but groaned and lay back. "Guessing my leg's broke."

Mrs. Vogel wiped his face with her apron. "I brought blankets. We'll slide you in the wagon and take you home. Dr. Jeffries will get you fixed up."

She stood, and we spread out the blanket. She took hold of Mr. Vogel under one shoulder. I took the other, and we pulled him onto the blanket. He cried out once, and I paused, but Mrs. Vogel spoke in a soothing voice to her husband and frowned at me. We didn't stop again until we'd reached the wagon.

Then we propped the boards from the ground to the wagon. I took one corner of the blanket, and Mrs. Vogel took the other. We pulled him up the makeshift ramp and into the wagon.

"Sit in back and try to keep him still," Mrs. Vogel commanded. Then she took the reins and urged the horses home.

When she pulled up in front of the barn, she turned to me. "I think we'll just lay him in the barn. Go make a big pile of straw in the empty stall. Then I want you to go to the Petersons. They have a phone, and they'll call Dr. Jeffries. Can you do that?"

I gulped. "Where do the Petersons live?"

"Past the schoolhouse about a mile. Turn right at the four corners. It's a big white house. Long driveway with maple trees."

I leapt from the wagon, ran into the barn, and threw straw down in a pile. Then we used the blanket to drag and carry Mr. Vogel into the barn. He groaned a lot as we moved him, but his eyes stayed shut.

"Go on, now." Mrs. Vogel waved, and I ran back to the wagon.

Edith and Forest did not want to leave the barnyard. After a day in the field, they expected their grain and a rest. I clicked my tongue, slapped the reins on their back, and shouted *giddyup* three times before they finally began walking down the lane. I slapped the reins on their backs, and they broke into a reluctant trot.

They settled down once we turned on to the road. We passed the schoolhouse in no time. Then at the place where the two roads intersected and formed four corners, I turned them again. I could see the house and the long driveway. We skidded into their driveway, and I pulled the team to a stop in front of the big white two-story.

Without pausing, I wrapped the reins around the brake, jumped from the wagon, and ran to the house. Then I pounded on the door and waited for someone to answer, trying to catch my breath and still my heart.

Mrs. Peterson opened the door. "Yes, may I help you?"

Before I could answer her, I heard a squeal. Then the thumping of feet on the stairs, and Emma threw herself in my arms. "Bert, what are you doing here?"

I hugged her tight for a second. Then prying her off me, I looked back up at Mrs. Peterson. "Mr. Vogel hurt his leg real bad out in the field. Can you call the doctor? Please?"

"Oh, my. Oh. Yes, I'll call Dr. Jeffries right away." She stooped down to my sister. "Emma, dear, go get your daddy from the barn." Then she hurried out of the room.

Emma gave me one more brief hug before skipping off toward the barn. Couldn't the girl just run for once?

In minutes Mrs. Peterson returned to say the doctor was on his way to the Vogels. Outside Mr. Peterson already sat on our wagon holding the reins.

As I climbed up to the seat, Mrs. Peterson promised to follow in the buggy with Emma.

When we arrived back at the Vogels, the doctor pulled up right behind us in his black automobile. Dr. Jeffries bounded out of the car carrying a black bag.

"He's in the barn," I shouted as I climbed down.

The doctor hurried off to the barn, followed by Mr. Peterson. I headed for the house. I could hear Bossy lowing. Milking time had passed, and she was letting us know.

By the time I got the clean milking pail, put grain in the bin, and let Bossy in her stall, they were carrying Mr. Vogel into the house. They'd strapped his leg to a piece of wood, and they were carrying him on a stretcher the doctor must have brought with him. I milked Bossy, turned her out, and fed the chickens and pigs.

By the time I'd finished, the sun had sunk behind the barn, and the shadows stretched long across the yard. As I entered the house, Mrs. Peterson stood at the stove stirring something in a big pot. Emma sat on a kitchen chair swinging her legs. She saw me and hopped up.

"Bert." She wrapped her arms around me.

"Hi, Emma." I hugged her back and then tiptoed into the front room. Mr. Peterson was sitting in Mr. Vogel's chair. I could hear a murmur of voices from the Vogels' bedroom.

"Will he . . . will he be okay?" I whispered.

Mr. Peterson looked up and smiled. "Yes, son. He'll be fine in a month or so. He broke that leg pretty bad, but the doctor's putting a cast on it. You did a good job. You're a hero, young man."

Slightly embarrassed, I wandered back out to the kitchen.

"Where do you sleep?" Emma danced around me.

"Mrs. Peterson, is it okay if I show Emma my room?" I asked.

She turned from the stove, wiping her hands on one of Mrs. Vogel's aprons. "Sure. Go ahead. But then come back down because we're going to have supper. We need to get our little Emma home to bed. She has school tomorrow, you know."

"Yes, ma'am." I climbed the stairs with Emma right behind me. She looked at my bookshelf, thumbed through the shirts and overalls in my closet, and sat and bounced on my bed.

"Where's your toys, Bert?"

I grinned at her. "I'm too old for toys. No time anyways. By the time I get done helping with all the chores, and we have supper, I'm ready for bed. Sometimes Mr. Vogel reads to us from the Bible, and sometimes I read books Miss Jones lends me."

"I'm glad I live with the Petersons. It's lots nicer there."

My grin turned to a scowl. I thought it was plenty nice here on the farm.

Just then Mrs. Peterson called up the stairs. "Emma, darling. Bert. Time for supper."

Everyone but Mr. and Mrs. Vogel was already seated at the table. Dr. Jeffries sat in my chair, so I took the one next to him. Mrs. Peterson served us chicken noodle soup she'd brought from her house. It tasted great, but I was so tired and so much had happened I just wasn't hungry. I chased the noodles around with my spoon, ate the pieces of chicken, and finally dropped my spoon. I knew you were supposed to eat what was served you, but the pigs would love leftover noodles.

CHAPTER 21

The next morning Mr. Vogel's voice didn't come booming up the stairs to tell me, "Time to get to milking."

I pulled on overalls and a shirt in the dark and tiptoed downstairs. Mrs. Vogel was in the kitchen. She looked like she'd slept in her clothes. Her hair stuck out all over, and the apron she wore had a streak of food from yesterday.

She handed me the milk pail. "Can you handle the chores by yourself this morning?"

"Sure." I took the pail and hurried out to the barn. I would have to work hard not to be late to school.

When I finished all the chores and carried the pail of warm milk inside, Mrs. Vogel had changed clothes and brushed her hair. "Mr. Vogel is awake. Would you like to take his oatmeal in to him?" She had a tray all ready with oatmeal, a piece of toast, and coffee.

I'd never been in the Vogels' bedroom. I lifted the tray. "Should I stay while he eats?"

"I think he can manage okay. You can put the tray on the nightstand. I put a bell in there, so he can let me know if he needs something."

I walked slowly, watching the cup of coffee so it didn't slosh over. When I entered the bedroom, Mr. Vogel used his arms to hoist himself to a sitting position.

"Morning, Bert. You got the job of waiting on the invalid, huh?"

His injured leg was stretched out in front of him. The cast made his leg look like a giant white sausage with toes sticking out at the end.

I stopped at the foot of the bed. "Does it hurt?"

"Not like it did last night. Thanks for all your help. You did a real fine job." He gestured at the leg. "Spring's not a good time for this to happen."

"It's okay. I can help. School will be over in just four days."

"Yes, that's so. I guess for a few weeks you'll have to be the farmer. Now what you got there on the tray?"

"It's oatmeal." I brought it up to the nightstand and shoved a photograph in a little gold frame back to make room. I handed him the bowl of oatmeal and the spoon. Then I took a closer look at the photo. It was a boy about my age dressed in overalls and a shirt. I recognized the shirt. It hung in my closet. Mrs. Vogel had given it to me the first day I came.

Mr. Vogel must have noticed me staring at the picture. "You're wondering who the boy is."

I nodded.

"That's John Arthur. He was our son."

I waited for him to go on, but he just sat there in bed, the spoon full of oatmeal dripping back in the bowl.

"What happened to him?"

"He got polio and died. Two years before you came." Mr. Vogel dropped the spoon back in the bowl. "We don't talk about him much, but we miss him."

Mr. Vogel looked down at his bowl and then he looked up at me and smiled. "We're mighty glad you're here."

Mrs. Vogel called from the kitchen. "Bert, you better get out here and eat your oatmeal or you'll be late."

Later as I walked to school, I thought about John Arthur and how I wore his clothes and slept in his bed and ate at his table. I felt a little sad, almost like I'd known him, and now he was gone. Then I remembered how Mr. Vogel said he was glad I was here, and I felt like skipping down the road like Emma did.

The schoolhouse was just coming into sight, when I heard the bell ringing. I sped up, sprinting down the road like I was crossing a New York street. As I ran into the schoolyard, I could see the last of the line marching in. I put my head down and imagined I was Forest, running to the barn. I slid into my chair just as Miss Jones said, "Good morning, class. Please stand for the Pledge of Allegiance."

I mouthed the words, trying to get enough oxygen in my lungs to breathe without panting. After the pledge, we sang, "My Country, 'Tis of Thee." Then Miss Jones gave assignments and called the first graders to the front.

After I pulled my reading book from my desk, I looked up. Miss Jones was standing by my desk. I expected a scolding or even some kind of punishment for being late. Instead she put a hand on my shoulder. "Emma told us about Mr. Vogel's accident. I guess this means you have extra chores in the morning."

"Yes, Miss Jones. I tried to hurry, but—"

"It's okay, Bert. If you are late, I won't count you tardy. Will you be able to come to the program on Friday?"

"I think so." I frowned and thought about how I could work it. "Maybe if I left school early so I could get the chores done before I came."

"That's fine. You may leave when you need to."

I flashed her my biggest smile. "Thanks."

Miss Jones tapped her finger on my book. "Now practice reading that story, so when I call the third graders up, you won't stumble over the words."

At lunch I'd sat beside Clarence on the grass when I spotted Frank. I braced myself for a whack on the head or a sneering comment. But he just passed by and said, "Hi, Bert. Hi, Clarence." I was so surprised I didn't say anything in response.

Then when we were playing baseball, he told me, "Good hit, Bert," even though someone caught it and I was out. That *do unto others* stuff must really work.

After school I didn't stay to work with Miss Jones, and I didn't waste any time. I just hurried back to the Vogels'.

As I trotted into the yard, I thought I saw a familiar blond head peeking out of the barn. I went to investigate. Sure enough, the blond dog was back. She wasn't dragging a rope this time. I dropped to the ground, and she waggled around me, cleaning my face with her tongue. I checked her neck, and the wound had healed some.

What were we going to do? How could I get her back to the Taylors?

I walked up to the house, the dog trotting behind. She curled up on the rug as I went into the kitchen. Mrs. Vogel already had a glass of milk poured for me and a cookie set out. I scooted my chair to the table and took a gigantic gulp of milk.

Mrs. Vogel walked into the room. "Roy is feeling much better today. Maybe after chores you can help me get him to the table, and we can all have supper together."

"Sure," I mumbled around my mouth full of cookie. "Uh, the dog is back."

She sighed deeply. "Well, we'll just have to keep her until Enos comes looking for her, or you and I can take the wagon over. I shouldn't have fed her so well."

"If I had the choice, I'd rather live here than with Mr. Taylor."

Mrs. Vogel laughed. "I guess I would too. It's too bad such a nice dog belongs to him."

I stuffed the last of my cookie in and grabbed the milk pail. "I'll get the chores done."

"Thanks. Oh, and Bert . . ."

I paused between the table and door.

"We got a letter today. Mr. Carter wrote that he would be here Friday afternoon."

My world turned upside down and inside out. I grabbed the milk bucket and hurried outside. On the way to the barn I kicked a rock, and the pain that shot through my big toe sent the tears streaming down my face. I'd known he was coming, but I'd stopped thinking about it.

The dog trotted after me into the barn. I knelt down and hugged her, pretending I was sad for her. Then I went through the motions I knew by heart. Let Bossy into her stall. Put food in the trough. Close the stanchion. Get the milking stool. Clean Bossy's udder. Watch the white milk foam into the pail. Some kids might call it work, but I loved milking. Gave me time to think and dream.

But today the thought of not doing this morning and night brought a fresh onslaught of tears. I blinked hard, but they still dribbled down my cheek. Without pausing in the rhythm of milking, I sniffed and wiped my face on the shoulder of my shirt.

How would Mr. Vogel do chores with a broken leg? Maybe they would let me stay until his leg healed. I knew better than that. It was a very long journey to New

York, and if Mr. Carter had traveled all this way to pick me up, he wouldn't leave without me.

After the milk pail was full, I let Bossy out and trudged through the rest of my chores. Then I washed my hands at the pump, and even though the water was cold I splashed it on my face and rubbed away the traces of tears. I didn't want the Vogels to think I was a sissy boy who cried.

With Mrs. Vogel on one side and me on the other, Mr. Vogel stepped and hopped to the kitchen. We maneuvered him to his chair, and he sank down, his white-sausage leg poking out in front of him. Mrs. Vogel had fried slices of ham, opened a jar of green beans, and there were biscuits. Just when I thought I couldn't eat any more, Mrs. Vogel asked, "Who wants a piece of chocolate cream pie?"

Of course I did.

After supper I fed the dog our scraps. Then Mr. Vogel read a little from the big Bible as Mrs. Vogel and I washed and dried the dishes. We helped him back into bed, and I went upstairs. I lay back on my pillow, and the thoughts tumbled around. I remembered the trip on the train and how I'd wanted only to protect my sister. Now she'd been adopted. In New York I wouldn't even see her. I turned my head into my pillow.

CHAPTER 22

The next morning I woke to the smell of sausage. Usually that meant biscuits and gravy for breakfast and a huge smile on my face. But not this morning.

I trudged through the chores with the dog at my heels. After giving her a plate of chunks of stale bread and some of Bossy's warm milk, I sat at the table.

Mrs. Vogel brought me a plate. She'd split two flaky biscuits and poured warm sausage gravy all over the top. "Breakfast for our hard-working boy," she said as she set it in front of me.

When she prayed, she thanked God for Mr. Vogel's good night. Then she added, "Thank you for Bert, who is helping out so much to keep the farm going."

"Amen," I mumbled as I dug into the first biscuit. "Do you want me to take a plate to Mr. Vogel?"

She shook her head. "He's still sleeping. Can you imagine that? He must be making up for that first night when he was in so much pain. Don't worry about him. You just eat your breakfast and get on to school."

As I eased the screen door shut behind me, the clouds that had blanketed the sky suddenly opened and rain

128

poured down. For a moment I wished I were Emma and could ride to school in a buggy with someone I called Dad.

I trudged along the muddy road. When I got to the schoolhouse, I was late. Everyone had already gone inside. I hung my jacket in the cloakroom and entered the classroom as quietly as I could, but my wet shoes made little squeaking noises. My pants were soaked, and my shoes dripped dirty little puddles on the floor.

"We're reading 'The Little Lost Dog,' " Clarence whispered. "Page 102."

I nodded and pulled out my reading book, but the words floated around the page like butterflies, and when Miss Jones called us up, I had no idea what the story was about. She seemed to understand my mood, and only called on me to read a couple paragraphs.

At lunchtime it was still raining. We all found places to sit around the classroom. I would have chosen a seat by the potbelly stove that occupied the center of the room, but it hadn't held a fire for several weeks. I still felt damp, and I shivered as I pulled out the cold potato and biscuit from my lunch pail.

Emma scrunched down between me and the bookshelf. "How's Mr. Vogel?"

"Better, I guess. He ate dinner at the table with us last night, and he slept late."

Emma peeled some of the crust off her white bread. She wouldn't have done that back in New York. "Mama says I'm going to take lessons and learn how to play the piano."

Trying to force some enthusiasm into my voice, I replied, "That's great." I knew I had to tell her about Mr. Carter coming, but the words stuck in my throat.

"I'm going to learn to play 'Baby Face,' and I'll play it for you."

The song I used to sing to her. I sighed. I had to tell her. "Emma, I know you'll be a great piano player, but I won't get to hear you. Mr. Carter is going to be here on Friday. I'll be going back to New York with him."

Instantly her big blue eyes filled with tears. "Why? Don't you want to stay in Iowa?"

"Course I do. I like it here. But when Mr. Carter left me, I heard him say I'd go back with him. I just didn't know when it would be. Now I know. He's coming Friday."

The tears spilled over, and Emma threw both arms around me. "No. I don't want you to go."

I gently pried her arms off. "You'll be okay. The Petersons adopted you. You have a family, and that's what we always wanted. I'll write to you, and maybe, when I get grown up, I'll ride the train and come visit."

Emma still snuffled as she poked things back in her lunch pail.

Miss Jones called out. "Who wants to play Hide the Thimble?"

The class became chaotic as the kids put away lunch pails and hurried to their desks. I didn't get another chance to talk to Emma.

As I left that afternoon, the gray clouds still pressed close, but no rain fell. I hugged my jacket around me and jogged most of the way home. I stopped on the porch to pet the dog. When I walked into the kitchen, Mr. Vogel sat at the table peeling potatoes.

"Afternoon, Bert. How was school?"

"Fine." I answered automatically. "How did Mrs. Vogel get you out here?"

"Dr. Jeffries stopped by and brought me a gift. Well, a loan really." He pointed, and there, leaning up against the wall, stood a pair of wooden crutches. "I can get around enough to help out again. I got tired of lying in that bed."

"That's great." I hoped I sounded sincere, but all it meant to me was that now I had no excuse to stay in Iowa. Mr. Vogel didn't need me to help. He could do it on his own.

He picked up another potato. "Enos Taylor stopped by today."

I froze. "Was he looking for his dog?"

"He was."

Had I dreamed she was on the porch? I glanced toward the screen door. "Why didn't he take her home?"

Mr. Vogel put a peeled potato in the big pot and grinned at me. "I said I might as well give him his asking price for the dog and keep her, since she seems to think she should live here."

"You did? She's your dog now?"

When Mr. Vogel nodded, I scrambled out of my chair and outside. Kneeling down, I hugged the dog tightly until she wiggled out and licked my nose.

"You'll love living here, girl. It's the best farm of all," I whispered in one soft ear.

CHAPTER 23

I woke Friday morning to a new sound. A kind of thump . . . scrape . . . bump . . . thump . . . scrape . . . bump. Then a familiar voice called up the stairs. "Rise and shine, boy. The sun'll be up any minute."

Mr. Vogel was at the stairway, using his crutches. I hopped out of bed and dressed completely before I remembered. Today Mr. Carter would come. And today I would leave to go back to New York.

In the gray light of the morning, I thumbed through my closet. I had the clothes I wore when I came on the train, and my favorite shirt, the one Mrs. Vogel sewed for me. The rest all belonged to John Arthur. I carefully folded the red plaid shirt and placed it on the dresser and put my copy of *Huckleberry Finn* on top.

Then I plodded down the stairs, picked up the milk pail, and headed out to the barn. Mr. Vogel sat on a bale of straw, his cast stretched out in front of him. He'd lit the lantern, and his face looked pale in the flickering light. Small beads of sweat stood out on his forehead.

"Hard work just getting to the barn." He gave me a little smile.

"Don't worry. You just sit. I can take care of things." I milked Bossy, fed the pigs, let the chickens out, fed them, and gathered eggs, aware of Mr. Vogel watching as I hurried about the barn. I picked up the full pail of warm milk. "You want me to help you get back to the house?"

Slowly he stood and propped the crutches under his arms. "No, you just get that milk in to the Missus and get your breakfast. Last day of school. You don't want to be late."

Last day on the farm too.

Mrs. Vogel took a fresh pan of biscuits from the oven. Eggs and slices of ham sizzled in their skillets. I washed my hands and face as she dished me up a plate. When I sat down, the screen door creaked, and Mr. Vogel hobbled in and sank into the chair. His crutches clattered to the floor.

This was my favorite breakfast, but I wasn't very hungry. As I nibbled on my biscuit, I had a new thought. *Would Mr. Carter take me before the program? Should I let Miss Jones know?*

"Um. Will I go to the program? I mean, with Mr. Carter coming."

Mrs. Vogel put her fork down. "Well, I hadn't thought of that. We don't know what time he'll be here, and he doesn't know about the program, but I think he'd want you to have the experience. We'll bring him along to watch if he's here for dinner. And he can leave after it's over."

"May I be excused?" I just couldn't force another bite of my breakfast down.

"You feeling okay?" Mr. Vogel asked.

Mrs. Vogel picked up my plate and scraped the left-over food into the slop pail. "You go on now. Your lunch pail is on the counter." As I hurried out the door, I heard her say to Mr. Vogel. "He's just all nervous about the program."

I made it to school while the kids were still milling around in the yard.

Emma skipped up and gave me a hug. "I was afraid you had already gone back to New York. Will you be here for the program? Will you, Bert?"

"Yes. I'll be here. I have to leave school early, so I can do chores before we come."

Miss Jones rang the bell, and we all lined up, buzzing like bees entering the hive. Miss Jones must have been in a really good mood, because she didn't once tell us to hush.

The morning went quickly. We didn't have any real assignments. We read, played some games, and had a spelling bee. Before I knew it, Miss Jones dismissed us for lunch.

She met me in the cloak room. "Be sure to be back here at 6:30. We'll eat first and have the program afterward. You remember your lines, don't you?"

When I nodded, she asked, "Will you participate in the program?"

I hung my head. "No. I still don't want to do it. I'll sing the songs, just not my piece."

Her lips made a firm line, but she said, "All right. That was our agreement."

I stuffed my things into my bag. Then I stepped out into the warm noonday sun. I waved to Emma and walked down the road, sometimes avoiding the puddles from yesterday's rain.

I'd made my way down most of the driveway when I spotted it. The same shiny black automobile that had brought me to the Vogels' two months earlier. Mr. Carter had arrived.

The dog frolicked across the barn yard, and I knelt to pet her. I could see Edith and Forest in the pasture. I could get on Edith's back and ride away or hide in the henhouse with the chickens. I shook my head and walked into the house.

Mr. Carter and Mr. and Mrs. Vogel were sitting in the front room. I put my lunch pail beside the sink. Their voices fell silent.

Then Mrs. Vogel called. "Bert, come in here and say hello to Mr. Carter."

My feet felt like two blocks of ice from the ice house. I dragged them into the front room. "Hello," I said as I studied the colors on the braided rug.

"Why, hello, Bert." Mr. Carter talked in the tone he always used with children when other adults were around. "I hear you have been excellent help here on the farm. Especially when Mr. Vogel had his accident."

I scuffed the toe of one shoe on the carpet. "I like the farm. Can I go do chores now?"

Mrs. Vogel looked at Mr. Carter. "Did you want to talk to Bert now?"

Mr. Carter shook his head. "No, we can talk later. I understand there's a dinner and program at the school tonight."

"Yes, sir," I muttered as I grabbed the milking pail and raced for the barn. The animals seemed surprised to see me so early. I had to go through the pasture and walk Bossy up to the barn. She didn't give as much milk as usual. The chickens didn't seem pleased at being shut in their house either.

When I finished chores and carried the milk to the kitchen, the Vogels were still in the front room chatting. I could hear Mr. Vogel's chuckle and wondered which of my escapades they were laughing at. Without speaking to any of them, I hurried upstairs and dressed in the pants and shirt I wore here. Then I stuffed the shirt Mrs. Vogel had sewn and patched for me, the book Miss Jones had given me, and my pocketknife into my book bag.

As I forced my feet to trudge down the stairs, I heard a knock at the kitchen door. Mrs. Vogel laid aside her sewing and opened the door. Mr. and Mrs. Peterson walked in with Emma between them.

I stood on the bottom step and clutched my bag to my chest. Suddenly the room was quiet, and everyone looked at me. I looked at Mr. Carter and squeaked out, "I'm ready to go."

Mrs. Vogel frowned. "It's not time for the program yet. And why are you wearing those clothes? They don't fit you anymore."

I bent over and looked. The ends of my pants were far above my ankles. But these were the clothes I wore when I came. What did she want me to wear? I held up the bag. "Can I take this with me?"

She shook her head as if she couldn't understand. "Take it where?"

I raised my voice as if getting louder could help her. "On the long ride back to New York with Mr. Carter."

There was half a moment of silence, and then bedlam broke loose. Everyone talked at once. Mrs. Vogel waved her hands, Emma burst into tears, and the Petersons shouted.

Mr. Vogel struggled to get out of his chair. I stepped over and gave him my shoulder to brace himself as he stood. Then his two pinky fingers went to the corners of his mouth, and a piercing whistle rocked the room. All the adults were instantly silent, only Emma snuffled a little.

"Why do you think you're going back to New York with Mr. Carter? Is that what you want?" Mr. Vogel asked.

Tears pricked my eyes, but I blinked them back, determined not to be a sissy boy even if I had to leave the farm. "Before he left, I heard Mr. Carter say he would take me back to New York with him the next time he came."

Mr. Carter frowned. "You must have overheard me explaining the contract to the Vogels'. If the guardians do not want to continue, then I would either find another placement or take you back to New York."

Mr. Peterson began shouting again. "That's why we're here. Emma explained the situation and told us how much she missed her brother, and we'd like to adopt Bert."

Mrs. Vogel's face registered astonishment, anger, and sorrow. "Adopt Bert? But we're his guardians."

I could feel Mr. Vogel's hand gripping my shoulder. "It seems there has been a misunderstanding here. We never meant for you to think we were going to send you back to New York. The missus and I love having you live here. You have brought joy to a home that had forgotten how to laugh. But we wouldn't want to stand in the way of you sharing a home with Emma either. I know you love her." He wiped his worn hand across his face, then looked at Mr. Carter. "What do we do?"

Mr. Carter frowned at me. "Have you thought this whole time that you would go back to New York?"

I nodded.

"Well, it appears you have two families willing to give you a home. What do you want?"

I looked up at Mr. Vogel, his hand still warm on my shoulder. Mrs. Vogel's eyes were full of tears as she gazed at me. Across the room both Mr. and Mrs. Peterson were smiling broadly at me. Emma sniffed away her tears and bounced up and down.

"Can . . . can I think about it?" My head spun and my heart sang. I had a family. But which one was mine?

Mr. Carter said, "Of course. We kind of put you on the spot here. But I do need an answer before I leave tonight."

Mrs. Vogel handed me the bundle she'd been sewing. "Go back upstairs and change. Here's a new short-sleeved shirt. And there are some new dress pants in your closet."

"Thanks," I took the shirt and raced up the steps. When I came down in the new clothes, they'd helped Mr. Vogel into Mr. Carter's car. I squeezed in beside him, and Mrs. Vogel sat in front holding the picnic basket on her lap.

It only took a few minutes to travel to school in the automobile. I felt like a bank president, stepping out of that shiny black car, wearing my new clothes.

We spread blankets out in the yard, and families grouped themselves and opened picnic baskets. They brought a chair out of the classroom for Mr. Vogel. The Petersons sat next to us, and I joined Emma on her blanket after I'd filled my plate from Mrs. Vogel's basket.

"Will you really be my brother again?" She whispered as she peeled the crust off a slice of bread.

"I'll always be your brother. No matter who we live with or what our last names are. Even if I went all the way back to New York, I'd still be your brother." Then I gave her a quick hug before digging into the fried chicken and my favorite biscuits.

When my plate was nearly empty, Mrs. Vogel started slicing a chocolate cake. I shook my head. "I'm too full." Full of butterflies, that's what I was.

Just then Miss Jones stood on the steps and rang the recess bell. "I need the children who are in the program to line up and come into the classroom. Parents, take your time to finish up. We will begin in fifteen minutes."

We raced to take our places in the line without the usual jostling and shouting. Inside we listened as Miss Jones went over directions. We'd practiced so many times, we knew this all by heart, but still we listened.

My heart was pounding so hard I thought it must sound like Edith's hooves on the packed road when she trotted to town. Out of the corner of my eye I could see parents filing in and sitting in desks and folding chairs that looked like they'd been borrowed from the church. Mr. and Mrs. Vogel took two seats right in the front row.

After we sang everyone clapped for a long time. I don't think anyone had ever clapped for me before. Then the kids began to say their parts. Sarah gave the introduction, Dorothy said her poem while looking at the audience, and then it was Emma's turn. She skipped up to the stage. She spoke loudly, just like Miss Jones had taught us. "My name is Emma Peterson."

If I said okay, I could be Bert Peterson. I could have new clothes for every day of the week, live on that big farm, and have lots of toys.

Clarence nudged me. "It's your turn."

Instead of turning and going to the back of the line like I'd planned, I walked slowly to the front of the room. I swallowed hard, then took a deep breath and let it out.

"My name is Bert Vogel. Well, not yet anyway, but I want it to be. And this is the Beatitudes."

I never missed a word. And when I was done, I didn't follow Miss Jones's directions. Instead of returning to the end of the line, I went right out into the audience. And while everyone clapped, Mr. Vogel hoisted himself to a stand, and both he and Mrs. Vogel hugged me. I was in the middle just like a piece of ham in a biscuit. And it felt wonderful.

In the distance I heard the mournful wail of the train as it approached Oak Hill. My long ride home was over.